THE TWO DISCIPLINES

"My father told me you're a chess champion," Phebe says. "Do they make mistakes?"

Her eyes are gray. I suppose they would be lovely if they weren't staring at me and surrounded by so much mascara. Isabelle wears it too. Whenever I see a tube of it in her bathroom, it makes my eyes itch.

"They do," I say. "It's often the only way to win. By someone else's mistake."

"Yes, I can believe that," she says. "I've always looked at a dancer's injury as a present to the rest of us."

I close the drawer I have been searching through, turn, and stand as tall as I can. Without my habitual slouch, we are the same height. I watch as we take a measure of each other. This is how I look at someone during a match. I see that she already knows me better than her father does. That we both have spent a lot of our lives anticipating the failure that comes hand in hand with winning. A slow, warning pressure starts along the right side of my neck.

OTHER SPEAK BOOKS YOU MAY ENJOY

Empress of the World	Sara Ryan
The House You Pass on the Way	Jacqueline Woodson
Life Is Funny	E. R. Frank
My Heartbeat	Garret Freymann-Weyr
The Outsiders	S. E. Hinton
Someone Like You	Sarah Dessen
Speak	Laurie Halse Anderson
A Step from Heaven	An Na
When I Was Older	Garret Freymann-Weyr

THE KINGS ARE ALREADY HERE

GARRET FREYMANN-WEYR

speak

An Imprint of Penguin Group (USA) Inc.

SPEAK
Published by Penguin Group
Penguin Group (USA) Inc., 345 Hudson Street, New York, New York 10014, U.S.A.
Penguin Books Ltd, 80 Strand, London WC2R ORL, England
Penguin Books Australia Ltd, 250 Camberwell Road, Camberwell, Victoria 3124, Australia
Penguin Books Canada Ltd, 10 Alcorn Avenue, Toronto, Ontario, Canada M4V 3B2
Penguin Group (NZ), cnr Airborne and Rosedale Roads, Albany, Auckland 1310, New Zealand

First published in the United States of America by Houghton Mifflin Company, 2003
Published by Speak, an imprint of Penguin Group (USA) Inc., 2004

1 3 5 7 9 10 8 6 4 2

LIBRARY OF CONGRESS CATALOGING-IN-PUBLICATION DATA
Weyr, Garret.
The kings are already here / Garret Freymann-Weyr.
p. cm.
Summary: Two teenagers, one obsessed with the world of ballet and the other
with that of chess, join together in a quest across Europe and begin
to learn not only how to connect with other people, but why.
ISBN 0-14-240207-9 (pbk.)
[1. Interpersonal relations — Fiction. 2. Ballet dancing — Fiction. 3. Chess — Fiction.
4. Self-actualization (Psychology) — Fiction. 5. Single-parent families — Fiction.
6. Europe — Fiction.] I. Title.
PZ7.W5395Ki 2004
[Fic]—dc22 2004041636

Printed in the United States of America

To my mother, Rhoda Ackerson Weyr
and my grandfather, Garret G Ackerson, Jr.
for more than my name.

PART ONE

MANHATTAN AND GENEVA, THEN

one

MY THOUGHTS COME AND GO. THEY ARE EVERYWHERE AND nowhere, often at the same time. Trying to keep hold of them is harder than holding my center of balance ever was. And that was impossible. No kidding. For months and then years, I would relevé, release the barre, and hear the teacher say, *Hold your center of balance.* My center of balance was always too far away from me to hold. And then, one day, my center of balance held. And has held. For three or four years now.

Unlike my thoughts, which suddenly come and go. As if they were pilots on the Concorde and endlessly delighted with the idea of flight. It is okay, even permissible, for an ordinary person's mind to wander on occasion. But I am a dancer. I am training to become a ballerina. I take seven ballet classes a week at the Academy. They are my life.

I've learned a few crucial things outside of class that concern dancers, dancing, triumph, and failure: Most people eat too much to dance. Good dancers carry their brains in their feet. This forces many to conclude that we are stupid, but we know we have a more useful intelligence. No one can dance and think of other things.

I wonder how I will become the exception to this irrefutable truth. For although I still go to class, I think of other things. Floor plans. Hair ribbons. Stained-glass windows. Zippers that hook. The Alps. Little dogs who bark ferociously and strain against their leashes as if they were five times bigger than they actually are.

Napoleon complex, Mama says. Amusing in dogs. Dangerous in men.

I start paying more attention to the things she says. I read her articles—whose deadlines totally shape our life—for the first time. They make a kind of sense above and beyond having been written by my mother. I ask her how she arrived at this or that conclusion. I don't know which of us is more surprised.

I can see in the mirror during class that my attention is slowly leaving my body. I have been the lead girl at my level for so many years that it takes me almost four months to understand what is happening. My feet no longer care about the right way to do a battement tendu. I myself am not as interested in the fact that there is a right way. What's next? I wonder with a mixture of panic and curiosity. Will I take my place at the barre only to find that I am now indifferent to the very existence of a battement tendu?

I don't mention any of this at home. I certainly don't bring it to the attention of my teachers. I can still *do* a battement tendu, which is what they see. That I no longer care so much is strictly between me and the mirror. When not thinking of other things, I dwell on certain unpleasant facts.

In less than a year, I will be eligible for workshop selection. If that goes well, I can audition for the Company. I might even be invited to join. Judging by the careers of those who have gone before me, I will stay in the corps for no more than two years. Soloist is the next step up. Principal dancer will be my final destination.

During the following twenty years, give or take a few, depending on injury, I will compete with around eleven other

4

principal dancers. We will battle one another for parts and time and attention. On stage I will dance the best ballets that have ever been made. I will have curtain calls and hear the cries of happy people calling out, *"Brava!"*

Or, of course, I could blow the workshop performance and never get invited to audition anywhere. Failure and Brava are equal possibilities. That's the way it is.

I am fifteen. I have been at the Academy since I was nine. On merit scholarship since turning twelve. How can I possibly know what will come of the *other things* that are currently renting space in my mind and feet?

Will stained-glass windows bring me more or less of what I have been training for ever since seeing *Swan Lake*? I was only seven when my father took me to the Royal Ballet in London. Until that night, I knew nothing of ballet. Not even *The Nutcracker*.

I spent the following two years taking lessons here and there before I entered the Academy. By twelve, I knew that this was the only place in the world to train for the only ballets worth dancing. Now all my certainty is gone. I can see it vanishing, but there is a lot of blurry vision about what might lie ahead.

At dinner one night I ask Mama when she knew she wanted to be a writer.

"Journalist," she says. "A clever journalist knows the difference. I'm not a writer."

I silently berate myself for not having avoided that little aside. If she stays up late sipping Scotch, she will read over her clippings and whisper to herself about her many short-comings. *Clever girl*, she will say. *Such a clever girl. Useless, witty, clever girl.* It's awful. How can you cheer up someone who thinks being clever and witty is useless?

She's not a big drinker or anything, but Scotch and late nights do not bring out her best. Unlike, say, wine and a good meal. No one is more beautiful or charming or useful than my mother under the influence of the perfect match of wine with food.

"Okay," I say. "Journalist, then. When did you know?"

"It was more a question of knowing that I would never be a good diplomat's wife," she says.

Mama's father was a diplomat. My father was a diplomat too. He retired early from the foreign service and is now the European director of an agency that helps refugees. He is nineteen years older than Mama. He was, before I arrived, a great friend of the family. My mother was certainly never his wife.

They never thought to marry, as their affair was largely accidental. Much in the same way I was. As they both have told me, *these things happen.* Mama's feelings about *these things* vary. Often, I am interested in how they change and why, but tonight I want to keep us on track.

"Well, when did you know that?" I ask. "How old were you?"

"Out of college. I must have been twenty or—let me see—no, I was twenty."

As late as that. Amazing. What in the world did she do with her time when she was my age?

"Something you want to tell me?" Mama asks, and I say no. We leave the conversation mostly unfinished, like our

6

dessert, which we put out onto fancy glass plates to enjoy the sight of more than the taste. We are in the habit, my mother and I, of looking at dessert.

She was as old as twenty? Twenty is impossible. I can't wait five years before deciding if I want to spend my life dancing. If I did, my chances of ever dancing well enough would be zero to none. If I want to dance, I need to put an immediate stop to the comings and goings of my thoughts. I allow myself a few more days of avoiding the real question: Do I want to dance? Of course. It's such a stupid question. It's like asking if I want to live.

My closet and my drawers are filled with leotards, tights, leg warmers, thin sweaters, my first pair of toe shoes, sewing kits, my current ballet slippers (two months away from wearing out) and toe shoes (two weeks away from being comfortable and therefore useless). I go to a school designed to work around my ballet class schedule.

My being unremarkable in history, math, English, chemistry, and Spanish is not only acceptable, it is what is expected from all the dancers. The teachers do what they can with us, but they know we sit in their classrooms reluctantly. All of the students there are training for something else. It's mostly dancing or music, although we have the stray acrobat or movie star (they never stay long). No one there would ask whether I want to dance. My presence means I do.

Except. Maybe not so much. I keep taking my place at the barre, and then one day what is visible to only me and the mirror becomes visible to the other girls. I can see it in their eyes; I am no longer the girl to beat. If I wait any longer, my teachers are going to notice. I might lose my spot in the summer intensive.

Panic sets in, chasing curiosity right off the stage. This is worse than the time they told me there might be something wrong with my feet. I had to see retired dancers, physical therapists, and a doctor before we found a set of exercises that made my feet as strong and flexible as the rest of me. I was the last girl in my level to get toe shoes and the first to get a scholarship. My shortcoming turned out to be an opportunity to show my teachers what I was capable of achieving.

If I am now in the process of becoming a regular girl, I promise myself not to go down without a fight. I make an appointment with the Academy's head of faculty, just as Mama did when I told her I wasn't getting toe shoes. Every battle a dancer faces needs a strategic plan. I tell my wandering thoughts to rise to the occasion. I am not going to abandon my life on their account.

10. b4 Be7 11. a3f5 12. Rc1 Bb7. It's always a fine day when I wake up with chess, even though for too many months now it's been fragments of the worst games I've ever played. A truly fine day is when I wake up with only clean parts from good games in mind. A less fine day and I wake with the memory of that afternoon. The one when I moved each game to a draw as my father watched. His fury grew as he slowly understood what I meant to do. A terrible day is when I wake to blankness. A day when I look at the ceiling and have to say my name, my age, and my ranking number before I can remember where in the world I am.

On those days, I'm very careful. More than usual.

Here, however, I never get confused. Never wake up terrified. There is sunshine everywhere except in the hallway and bathrooms, which have no windows. Mr. Aldrich is quiet, a quality I value more than kindness, although I suppose he is that as well.

Every morning I am up first. I make toast and soft-boiled eggs. He says the coffee I attempt is too strong for him and that I am not here to make his breakfast. I worried he would forbid it, but I think he understood right away that there are certain things I have to do. I have been preparing breakfast since my mother determined I could do so without scalding myself. Now is not the time for a change.

After he showers and selects a tie, Mr. Aldrich makes the coffee. While I clean the dishes, he puts together a sandwich for my lunch. Unless the school called him at the office and told him, he seems to have known intuitively that I don't eat with the others. It's very hard for me to swallow in front of strangers—one quirk among many which I imagine my father is glad to have left behind.

Tests are approaching. They will determine my suitability for University.

"I'm not going," I have told him. As well as the numerous teachers, lawyers, evaluators, and administrators. "It's not in the plan."

The others look pained when I say this. They know the plan is my father's creation. *Monstrous*, I have heard them call it. They also use this word to describe him. People believe that without my father, I will pack it in. If they knew more about chess and were less worried about me, I would not have to see their pity. Mr. Aldrich is different, though.

"It's just a formality, Nikolai," he says. "Think of it as someone else's game."

I endeavor to do that. It's new behavior to go along with my new name. I have always been called Kolya. My passport and my official papers, however, all carry the name Nikolai Sergeyevich Kotalev. During my first few months here I was too exhausted to explain that my family and my acquaintances never used Nikolai, preferring the more familiar Kolya. And then it made no sense to announce that I was accustomed to answering to another name.

On the day that is exactly eight months after my father and I parted company, Mr. Aldrich asks if I want to take a look through some books he has. From two boxes in the small room where we play, I find a treasure trove of chess books. I know he wishes me to understand that he is glad I am here. We met at the British Consulate when I finally called attention to my father's absence. I was surrounded by new and strange grownups, but Mr. Aldrich immediately struck me as the most sensible.

He paid outstanding bills, saw to my visa, and offered me my first meal in countless days. When I moved into his spare bedroom, he was able to make it seem as if I were doing him the favor. We both needed company and were loath to ask for it. Chess is full of men whose lives have brought them to some sort of loneliness. Lonely people are (peculiar as it may seem) often the best company.

The chess books in Mr. Aldrich's possession are full of

games, analysis, forgotten endings, and obscure variations I have never seen before. It's also been eight months since I've had any word from Stas Vlajnik, who promised to take me as a student if I extradited myself from my father's grip. Mr. Aldrich is more concerned with the silence from Stas than with the passage of time measuring my father's absence. Thus the books.

"These are . . . stunning," I say, pleased to have found a word. English often lacks the structure I want to express myself. An adjective is not right. The books are more like an event, but *stunning* will go far to convey my meaning.

"I'm sorry I can't give them to you," he says. "They belong to my daughter."

Up until this moment I had not known he was a father. It is unlikely that this has been an oversight on my part or accidental on his. I am aware that people think I am preoccupied solely with chess, but this is not my luxury. As soon as my father and I left home, I had to study the how and why behind what other people did, thought, said, and believed. My father claimed not to care about others, but I knew our survival would depend on my caring and on his acting as if we did not. In this way, we guided each other.

I wonder what it is Mr. Aldrich wants me to know about his previously unmentioned daughter. The trip he took the week between Christmas and New Year's makes a new kind of sense. It's as if I'm looking at a piece on an unprotected square. If your opponent is clever, it's not there by accident. I see familiar flashing lights and the old *proceed with caution* warning from several hundred blunders and a thousand brilliant moves.

"But I can read them?" I ask.

"Yes," he says. "Take your time. Put the useful ones in your memory."

"Do you have a picture of her?" I ask, discarding numerous other questions. Parents in the West, I have observed, carry photographs of their children and like nothing more than to show them.

Mr. Aldrich opens his wallet. There is a picture of a girl. It serves me best to believe they all look the same. It is one of many ways I use to keep from thinking of them at any length; they have the power to harm concentration. On the back, he has written her name and age.

"I thought there was an *o* before the *e* in Phebe," I say.

"Usually, yes," he says. "Her mother named her for her own mother, but dropped the *o* so that Phebe would have a life unburdened by legacy."

I don't say anything. A response is not required. I had to teach myself this lesson, which is contrary to the rules of chess. A movement (a word, a gesture, a look) does not always mandate a countermove, -word, -gesture, or -look.

"Phebe Knight," Mr. Aldrich says. "Her mother sometimes calls her Day. 'From the night, will come the day.' I call her only by her name. The given one."

I wait again, but that's all. He's done, and the way he spoke of them—his daughter and her mother—made me think of pieces isolated within an opponent's fortress. I consider the topic closed and study his daughter's books until we retire for the night.

TWO

MY MEETING WITH THE HEAD OF FACULTY GOES BOTH BETTER AND worse than I had anticipated. My mother is already in the office when I arrive. I stand in the door, amazed and afraid. André Rogovsky, who governs the world in which I live, motions for me to sit down. I know he strikes many people as brusque as he doesn't do the pleasantries often used in conversation. "Time conspires against us," he likes to say.

"I was impressed by your initiative, Phebe," André says now. "Most girls in your situation would have waited for me to summon them."

"What is my situation?" I ask, sitting next to Mama, wondering why she didn't tell me she would be here. Is it already worse than I thought?

"I've had reports from two of your teachers," André says. "Mentally you've gone past what your body is ready for, and so you're bored."

"I'm not bored," I say quickly.

Many, many people would like my place at the Academy. It would be a crime for me to be bored. It would be rude. And it is an inaccurate description of the perplexed frenzy up in my head.

"You're not as interested as you could be," he says. "Should be."

"I know," I say. "It just happened. It's not on purpose."

"No one thinks it's willful," Mama says. "That's why André called me. To determine what it is you want."

"What it is she needs," André says.

"Are you going to throw me out?" I ask.

As far as I know, parents get called in only when you are invited to join the Company or asked to leave the Academy.

"You're much too talented to be shown the door," André says.

This would make me feel incredibly good if I didn't know that talent isn't all I need. There's dedication, discipline, zeal. Without that *will*, talent takes you nowhere.

"Unless you want to leave," Mama says.

"I am, of course, familiar with your mother's opinions," André says.

Mama is not a big believer in the merits of dance. She thinks the Academy's schedule narrows my life and limits my options. Any life, she says, that can accurately be described as a beautiful tragedy is not one to covet. *But it is your life,* she will say. *You choose as you must.*

"I don't want to leave," I say, more to her than to him.

"We could promote you early," André says. "It's a way to engage your interest, but almost certainly a route to injury."

A promotion means I would now have nine classes a week instead of seven. Nine classes a week. Do I want to take nine classes a week? I can answer that with a *no* since at this point I barely want to take seven. But this firm and clear *no* does not point to what I do want. Might want, instead of, say, nine classes.

"Is there another way?" I ask them.

"You take a break," André says.

"Look around and see what interests you," Mama says.

"I have to take class," I say firmly. "I can't not come to class."

Inexplicably, this is more true than my not wanting to take nine classes. *I have to take class.* Even if I spend all of it thinking of other things. I could never *not* come to class. For all the times that I am thinking of floor plans and hair ribbons, my body works on, hoping for its small, important glories.

The moments when I can feel just how much my turned-out feet depend on my hips. How during a port de bras, my fingertips and neck extend from a place deep inside my shoulders. How I am all of one piece. How I fit into the world. If it weren't for class, I would never get out of bed. What would be the point?

"Of course you must take class," André says. "But perhaps not here. After all, this is not a factory. You are not a product."

"André told me you might thrive in a different atmosphere," Mama says.

No one skips the summer intensive before their workshop year. No one. I am being thrown out. Why don't they just say that?

"Where else could I go?" I ask.

"Yes, this is a problem," André says. "Most of the schools in this country are pale imitations of what we have."

I can see pride in the truth of this statement leaking from his eyes.

"How would you feel about spending the summer with Clarence?" Mama says.

"In Switzerland?" I look at her and she nods yes. "For the whole summer?"

My parents don't have a custody arrangement. It's casual while also being set in stone. He visits New York for ten days in the fall and the spring. I spend the week between Christmas and New Year's with him, as well as two weeks in August. I like my father, and Mama claims to admire him.

We are agreed, however, that he has little in common with our lives. Mama has always said that Clarence is enjoyed most in small doses. What on earth has made her consider such a change in their carefully negotiated schedule?

"I've contacted an old friend," André says finally, interrupting our private, charged silence. "She has a studio in Geneva. She will take you in hand."

"Did you ask Clarence?" I ask Mama, knowing that of course she did. It's not the kind of detail she'd leave undone.

"He very much hopes you'll want to come," my mother says.

"I don't speak French," I say, wondering how I can thrive in a different ballet school without understanding anything above and beyond the names of the steps.

"You're not going away to make friends," André says. "Unless you'd like that to be the reason you are preoccupied."

Of course he means boys. They are the usual culprit. They are what cause girls with graceful necks and perfect turnouts to vanish. Back outside into life. It's always so sad. There was a boy about a year ago, but I found him . . . lacking. If I go outside into life, it won't be because of a boy.

"What if I fall behind?" I ask, wanting to go, but also afraid. Not of staying with my father, but for my body, which is trained to take class *here*. Not being here could wind up costing me something fierce and precious.

"You will catch up," André says.

"Or you'll fall into something else," Mama says.

I look up at her sharply. I am not going if that is what she has in mind. Forget it.

"There are ways of letting the mind wander while the body keeps working," André says. "It is not *my* plan for you to fall into something other than your dancing."

He stands up, looking through my mother. We're done.

"Thank you," I say, hoping I will still mean it when I return.

"Not at all," he says, his shoulders making a slight, matter-of-fact shrug. Although André is long retired, in his slight movements one can often see whole performances.

Mama had hoped to take vacation time in July and meet me in Rome. But she has a new, big deadline. A profile on three radio talk show hosts. She will have to travel to Ohio, Indiana, and Kansas. Although she works for a magazine about the city, she often writes articles about places far away from it.

When I was little, she worked for a wire service. We moved a lot and her assignments were dictated by news events. For the past six years we have lived only in Manhattan and her assignments have been dictated by her editors. Or her interests that pass editorial approval. I don't ask if her editor or her own interest has sent her in the opposite direction from my destination.

I will see her in August. In Rome. We will have a good time. But not until two months have passed.

"I will always be no more than a phone call and a flight away," Mama says as we try to pack a summer's worth of clothing and dance gear into a reasonably sized bag.

"I know," I say, reluctantly removing some items from my piles. I'm going to do more washing by hand than usual and have only two dresses to choose from instead of five.

"Let Clarence help you as much as you can bear it," she says. "It's all he wants. And his intentions are good."

"I know," I say, more worried that neither of them is going to be very useful if I spend the summer taking class from a stranger and return still no longer the girl to beat. Still more occupied with my thoughts than the right way to do a battement tendu.

"Don't be too strict with yourself," Mama says. "If something comes up that conflicts with your class schedule, let it."

I'm not even going to have this conversation. If I tell her that nothing but my class schedule matters, she will ask how I can know that. I used to tell her I just knew, but since I don't know what I once did, I let her give me the speech about a full life.

"I'll miss you very much, Mama," I say when we finally shut the suitcase. This, at least, is certain and true.

I have to move. The closed topic is approaching.

"It's just for the summer," Mr. Aldrich says. "Normally she comes for only two weeks in August. I'm more surprised than I can say."

He looks frightened and startled, not surprised. I wish I could do something for him. In the meantime, I am glad to own only one suit, two pairs of pants, two shirts, one sweater, a T-shirt (it was a present), two pairs of socks, and two sets of pajamas. Also a tie, which my father left behind in our rented rooms. It is the one I always borrowed when I wore the suit.

Everything fits into my small, hard case. The handle is broken, but no matter.

"Isabelle will be very glad for your company," he says.

Isabelle Craig is his lady friend. She works for one of the UN agencies. Unruly hair, billowy skirts, shawls, silver bracelets. A bit messy.

"And her apartment is much closer to the city center than mine."

It's dark at Isabelle's. And her only view is a glimpse of Lac Léman, not the frontal assault on Mont-Blanc that Mr. Aldrich has. How did I miss this? I don't like her. I almost never waste energy liking or disliking people. It wastes time. Isabelle is what my father would call a real piece of work. His English remained borderline throughout our three years of shared "freedom," but he was fluent in all the words and phrases used to put women down.

"Yes," I say. "It is. I am most grateful. She knows this?"

"There's no need for gratitude," he says. "Isabelle is relieved to be of use. She still feels badly about how that other bit turned out."

She tried to get me a job for the summer. Something useful and interesting. A job to help me get on in life. I did well on all those tests, and she thinks it's a crime that I won't even consider University. So while she was on the verge of mobilizing her networks to find me something, I got a job in a hotel restaurant.

Dishes, dishes, dishes. Busy hands, empty mind. Mr. Aldrich understood. Isabelle, who says I make her feel ancient by calling her Miss Craig, felt terrible. And now I will live with her, and the daughter will live here.

"I wish she didn't," I say. It will not be good for me to be in such close proximity to someone who feels badly about how she treated me. Concern I can handle. Also anger, rage, or despair. Guilt and worry are not my specialties. They were my mother's. When she left us, she took them away along with her clothes and books.

"What about the tournament?" I ask him, humiliated at having to ask but knowing I must.

"I will expend every effort in that direction," he says. "If I can't accompany you, arrangements will be made. You won't go alone. Or unprovided for."

It's only a variation, I tell myself. No more, no less. The plan is still the same. I will enter and do my best (enter and *win*, my father would have insisted; perhaps his is the better way) at the tournament, achieving what I need to in order to qualify for Salzburg. I might receive word from Stas while there. If not, it will help prepare me for my return to Salzburg.

Where my life blew apart last year. By my own hand. My father wanted me to win there so that I could earn my grandmaster title. I had been the under-eighteen Soviet champion by the time I was twelve, and he saw no reason I couldn't be a grandmaster by fifteen. Then we would go to America. I had always done what my father planned. There were certainly times when I could not think well or was outmatched, but the consequences were always so ugly (screaming, furniture breaking, and so on) that I studied and played my way to triumph more often than not.

Chess is a small world. A whisper in Yugoslavia resonates from California to the Urals. I heard what people said. That my father held me back. That he didn't know anything about chess. That his paranoid claims of other grandmasters stealing my ideas made it impossible for anyone to teach me.

All true. But all missing the bigger picture. With my father breathing fire down my neck, I never had to waste time or energy motivating myself to study endgame positions. I kept myself drilled until I could tell at once if it was a draw or a win. I have never longed for a life outside the board. The sound of children playing or whatever it is they do fills me with both terror and contempt.

During tournaments, I had to fear my father's inevitable wrath (directed at me, my opponents, their trainers, other parents), but it made my vision sharper and my game as clear as glass. As an added benefit, I never had to think about what I would eat, when I would sleep, if I would play. He did all that. Far longer than was necessary.

At least, I assumed it was long past necessary until I contemplated doing it on my own. I suppose I had been hoping that Mr. Aldrich would do a lot of the detail work for me this summer. Minus the sound and fury, of course. Now I will have to rely on other arrangements. Only a variation, I repeat, wondering where I put my case when I first unpacked in this bright, white room with twin beds covered in matching blue spreads.

"We will find him, Nikolai," Mr. Aldrich says.

Although I know he does not mean my father, but the everelusive Stas Vlajnik, who is far more crucial to my game, I can feel a burning in my throat, nose, and eyes. Tears. More than anything else, my father kept these at bay. I never cried. Not when my mother left us. Not when my headaches started going from bad to worse. Not even at that awful game in Salzburg.

"I know," I say. "It will happen."

Yet, right now I would ask for my father. Beg for my father. He would freeze these burning things. He would, he could, with only a careless glance, return me to my sharp, clear habits. Stas, whom I want and need to find, could hardly be as useful as my father would be at instantly drying up this peculiar aspect of grief.

THree

MY FATHER LIVES IN A NEAT, WELL-FURNISHED APARTMENT WITH terraces outside all the windows and two sinks in the bathroom next to the bedroom he sleeps in. The bathroom next to the guest room, which I have agreed, over the years, to call *my room*, has only one sink. It also has a bidet. Good for washing out tights and leotards.

I first came to visit when I was seven. My grandfather took me to JFK and handed me to a flight attendant, who promised to keep an eye on me and find my father once we landed at Cointrin. I probably was allowed into the cockpit and given extra sodas. Somewhere I still have the plastic envelope I wore around my neck as I crossed and re-crossed the Atlantic. It held my passport, my ticket, and five hundred Swiss francs.

Clarence, who has always requested that I call him by his first name, didn't meet me until I was three. In fact, he didn't even know I existed until I was two. He heard it from a friend of my grandfather's. It was at a cocktail party in London.

It took Clarence a year after that party to ask Mama if he could be a part of my life. And that's how I would describe him: a part of my life. If my father had been somebody else, Clarence also would have been a part of my life. He and my grandfather were once best friends. I'm not sure when that ended or even why. I have guessed it was due to how *these things happen*, but I might be wrong.

For the record, the only bad thing I ever heard my

grandfather say about Clarence concerned his living in Geneva. "A city suitable only for bankers, rare book dealers, and foreigners," he said. And, of course, the occasional dancer who has lost her way.

The studio where André's old friend will take me in hand is in walking distance from Clarence's office. He lives in Chêne-Bougeries, uphill from the city itself. So in the mornings, we take the number 12 tram from the apartment into Geneva. We get off near the Jardin Anglais. He walks me to the flower clock so I can admire it and the view it affords of swans on Lac Léman and of the Jet d'Eau, which is the world's tallest fountain and one of my top five favorite things. These are all places we looked at when I was a little girl and Clarence was trying to make each day I spent with him be like a postcard.

The woman who runs the studio is not, as I had assumed she would be, a retired dancer from the Company at home. Her name is Elena Holmes and we call her Mademoiselle. We start each class making our révérence (the formal thank you) instead of ending class with it, as I have been taught. Although she doesn't stress speed and clarity as much as we do at the Academy, Mademoiselle is not a bad teacher. She is also pretty nice, letting me stay afterward so I can do extra barre work for strength and an adagio on pointe.

The studio is not a professional school, and I don't think the other students have serious dance ambitions, but I refuse to worry. Back at the Academy, André planned for me to be *here* so as to return to dancing at the top of my level *there*. My job, as I see it, is to get my thoughts back into my body. It's often close to impossible, especially during the extra barre time, when I'll realize that I'm not even looking in the mirror to check myself. It's scary and it keeps happening.

The girls at the studio are all incredibly small, fine boned and thin. I'm at least three inches taller than everybody else. And I have breasts compared to them. This is an unwelcome shock. I know it has more to do with my build than my success or failure as a dancer, but still and all. I have never been the biggest girl in a room, and I am not thrilled that this has changed just because I have switched parents.

Some days I walk over to Clarence's office and wait for him. We go back home for lunch and then he returns to work. In the evenings, we cook or walk to a place nearby that he likes a lot. The first week I am here, Clarence has tickets for events every night. Open-air concerts, one at Victoria Hall, movies at a converted old factory, theater, and dance. It is a touring modern dance troupe at the Grand Théâtre that makes me beg for a break.

"I hate the way they roll around the floor," I say. "It's unsightly."

"We can leave," he says. "There's no rule that says one has to return after intermission."

"There's no rule that says we have to go out," I say. "What do you do at night?"

"I am very dull," he says. "But this is your visit and we will shine."

"I'm here for almost three months," I say. "I don't think we can call it a visit."

"Very dull," he says as we head for his car.

"Dull is Mama on deadline," I tell him. "Don't worry about it."

He decides that we will go to distant cities on the weekends. It will brighten up my stay to travel out and about, he says. It's impossible, as I have a class on Saturdays, but still I let him show me maps, brochures, and train schedules. It is the least I can do.

It is a technicality tournament. No one is pleased that I am here. It's not fair to the other players. My ranking makes it ridiculous for me to compete for the Swiss National Youth Champion title. Not to mention, I didn't even play in last year's Under-eighteen Geneva Open. I will face the winner here. An exception has been made. Rules have been broken. I need a champion title to go back into the Salzburg round robin, and no stringent scholastic tournament will have me back.

There is a raging and legitimate debate in certain places about my actual academic achievements. The school my father claims I graduated from says I never finished. This is exactly why I have been doing time at the International School in Geneva and why I took those tests. Until Mr. Aldrich can get the papers through the right channels—"Chess organizations have more bureaucrats than the foreign service," he has said more than once—the Swiss Youth title is the solution. Unless I am prepared to wait a year.

I am not.

"They should just give the title to you," Isabelle says during a break between rounds on the first day. "No one here wants to play you. My God, you should hear what they say."

"I have heard," I tell her. I am lying on the floor of her hotel room with a cold, wet washcloth over my eyes. Isabelle is convinced that cooling my eyes in this manner three times a day will make me less vulnerable to migraine. She had them while in her twenties and considers herself a bit of an expert. I don't know that I value her theories highly, but I have found that it is easier to do as she wishes than to resist.

"Even the ones who say you play like a machine say you don't have what it takes," she says. "Everyone has an unsolicited opinion of your training."

This is fairly common at tournaments. I myself have unsolicited opinions about who trains and how. We know one another's games by reputation and results. We are ranked against one another and given a number based on how we play. Not to judge others would be foolish.

"Do you know they all call you Kolya?" she asks from the bed to which she has retreated, a pillow under her knees, her bracelets clinking gently when she moves.

"Yes," I say. "It was my name from home, but I prefer Nikolai."

"The whole building is crawling with freaks," she says. "Freaks praying for you to lose."

"My father did not make me a lot of friends," I tell her, hoping that she does not go on in this vein for much longer. I am playing inside of beautiful patterns and having a good time. I do not want to be in Zurich in the company of a woman who thinks I am the King Freak. It's not that her opinion matters, but I don't wish to know it.

"Nikolai, I'm sorry," she says. "I forgot. Forgive me."

"It's nothing," I say, meaning it. She'd have to do a lot worse to me than that to need forgiveness.

Isabelle spends a few more days watching all the crying kids, angry parents, and furious teachers. The people trying to get me thrown out and the people who want to know who my teacher is. Where my father, whom they know by sight or story, has gone to. And then she's had it. She tells an angry father that if his son was crying, it wasn't my fault, but the fault of lousy genetics.

She begins to court the judges and the men I have identified as grandmasters of note. She also lingers with the grandmasters I told her had hit their peaks decades ago. The men who no longer have an eye on their own futures but are making judgments about chess and its future.

In the evenings, she has copies of great games from times gone by and/or variations on positions from games I have played that very day. I quickly come to understand that Mr. Aldrich's lady friend might be a real piece of work, but she is also what I have heard men call a *dish*. She claims that her charms have nothing to do with this bounty of information.

"You should hear them," she says. "Ideas, theories, concepts. They can't get them out fast enough. It's as if they've been waiting for years to help you."

"Isabelle, we don't know these people," I say.

I know she means well and it could all be harmless, but there's no way to test it. I know a man who tried to give my father copies of the openings his own son had spent all summer devising with his teacher. My father burned them in the bathtub, but it turned out the father had wanted his son to leave the game. They had been the real deal.

On a much grander scale, there are the well-known stories of the two men currently vying for world champion. One wins the title, three years later, the other takes it back. I think of them as two Kings, never moving from either E8 or E1. The one who is a good Soviet citizen spends a lot of time and money bribing the other one's trainers. So the other one rotates his seconds and trainers every year. He sacrifices consistency for safety. I try to explain all this to Isabelle.

"You mean people cheat?" Isabelle is incredulous.

There is a reason I do not talk about chess to people who are outside of it.

"People use different maneuvers on and off the board," I say.

Our meal arrives. She has been quite good about my not wanting to eat in the dining room. It took her five years of traveling for work before she could eat alone in public.

"I don't think these men have it in for you," she says. "They say that with your father gone, there is no stopping you."

"Stopping me from what?"

"Other titles. Including world champion."

She needs to be cured of this, and quickly.

"Isabelle, I am not interested in becoming world champion. I want to play in order to play well," I say, fighting to stay calm. "In order to play beautifully. It happens that the result of this involves winning, but it is not the point. It is not why I play."

"I didn't know," she says, and then, after a bit, "How can I help you?"

No one has ever asked me this before at a tournament. Although I know Mr. Aldrich wouldn't need to ask the question (he'd know), I'm glad to have her here.

"By letting me play," I say. "The fact that you are having a good time. It all helps."

"He made you play to win," she says.

Of course my father made me play to win. But there is more to it than that. He made me play for money. He made me play to live. He made me play because he knew I could and because he loved me.

"He also turned me into someone who can play well," I say. "Often, quite well."

"I see," she says, and while I know she doesn't, I sense that she wants to. That she's curious. I am in no danger of being a freak in her eyes. It still doesn't matter, but it's nice. I'm truly grateful and hope one day I will be able to express this.

four

One afternoon, as we are finishing lunch, I mention that I might ask Mademoiselle if I can help her with the classes she gives for the little girls. At a certain age, I say, there is no replacement for having your hand or leg or shoulder *put* into place. I could do as little as that even if I can't talk to them.

"Although it feels as if everyone here speaks better English than I do."

"There is an emphasis in some schools on foreign language," Clarence says.

"No kidding," I say. "There's not one girl at the studio who can't ask me eighteen questions about the Academy. All in English."

"Do you read?" Clarence asks.

"I know how," I say, resigned to the way this talk will go. "I'm sure Mama has told you I don't read enough."

"She tells me very little," he says. "Come, I have something for you."

There is a small room between my father's room and the guest room. It has a narrow desk, many shelves, and a large number of brown boxes. Clarence is seldom in here, and I have poked around in it only once or twice.

"When your grandfather died, his estate was in some disarray."

I nod, thinking that this is, at best, an understatement. My grandfather was sixty-seven when he had a massive heart attack. Since I was only nine, a lot of that time is blurred. But I clearly remember my mother as tired, shocked, and drinking Scotch late at night. She was planning a huge memorial service and then a bigger party at my grandfather's house near Gramercy Park, which would have to be sold to help settle the estate.

There was no will—only some notes Mama could make no sense of. Any spare moment she had was spent trying to locate the lawyer and avoiding her brothers and their helpful suggestions for a woman in her situation, or, as they insisted on calling her, *an unwed mother*. When my grandfather was alive, he had protected Mama from my uncles and their opinions. He had also kept *them* from knowing that he often gave her money.

The money was to help her raise me, but still and all. My uncles had kids too. Albeit kids with no real ambitions beyond having regular lives and with mothers who did not work. The money Mama got was to help her hire babysitters or to work only part-time. He sent money from his different posts—Prague, Budapest, and Warsaw—before retiring to New York. When her brothers finally found out, they resented it.

As the memorial service drew near, no one was happy and no one knew quite what to do.

Clarence arrived. As a friend of the family, he knew my grandfather's lawyer well. The estate was settled to everyone's satisfaction. Clarence put Mama's brothers, whom she now insisted on calling *very married,* onto planes back to their Midwestern cities.

There were a few more loose ends, and then he himself was gone. Mama said he had to learn that he couldn't possibly be her father and mine at the same time, which I accepted as a reasonable statement. Clarence, according to my mother, did not take it as well. It's safe to say disarray hung over us for a year. Maybe two.

"Alexander left his books to me," my father says now. "The note said I should hold them until such time as you might express an interest."

I look at the boxes piled under and around the narrow desk and along Clarence's bookshelves. There are a lot of them. What does one do with all these books? Once they have come out of all these boxes?

"I realize that you haven't expressed an interest," he says. "But until you know that they are yours, how will you know to ask for them?"

"Why you?" I ask. "I mean, why not ask Mama to hold them?"

"I can't be certain, of course," Clarence says. "But I think he felt badly about how things played out."

"What things?" I ask.

"I have liked having them here," he says. "Waiting for you. In that way, they have kept me company."

"Have you read them?" I ask, wanting to know what kind of company a bunch of old books can possibly be.

"Some," Clarence says. "He and I had divergent interests."

"What things?" I ask. "What was played out?"

"You really don't know," Clarence says. "I'm surprised."

I wait. Unlike Mama, who has a ready answer for me at all

times, Clarence needs to consider if he has the right to answer my questions.

"Your mother didn't think I should come and live nearby," he says. "It was only at Alexander's insistence that I was allowed to visit. And, eventually, that you were allowed to come here."

I know a version of this. But in it, my mother said no because she thought he'd smother us. It was only after doing an article about girls lacking father figures that she asked her father to give Clarence the go-ahead.

"Whenever I raised the issue of moving to be near you, Maggie said it was impossible," my father says. "I think it is possible Alexander regretted all of this."

Regretted? Something Mama did? I don't think so. My grandfather always told me that, under the circumstances, my mother had handled everything with both grace and cleverness.

"Your mother made excellent decisions about difficult things," my grandfather said.

He made me repeat it so that I would be prepared for people's stray and/or rude comments—silly things, like *out-of-wedlock* or *bastard*. Things that no one cares about, but which mattered a lot to my grandfather and his friends at the time when my mother and Clarence had their accidental affair. We didn't know that I was going to vanish into a life where no one cared where you came from above and beyond where you learned to dance.

Excellent decisions about difficult things. I never needed to say it, but I never forgot from whom I had heard it and why.

And yet here are all these books. Given over to my father

to hold in custody. Not to my mother. What did Alexander, as Clarence calls him, want me to know about how things played out?

When we return to Geneva with a small monetary award and a title, I decide that with the money saved from my hotel job I can afford to join the city's chess club. My father always objected to these places on the grounds that my study habits and playing strength could be too easily observed. Why pay, when for free I could sit at home, read, memorize different variations, or walk myself through the most difficult, most beautiful games ever to see the light of day?

Why, indeed?

Well, for one thing, it's easier to study in a room devoted to chess than any place I can find in Isabelle's small, dark apartment. For another, if I want a break from my books and my mental exercises, there is always someone here happy to play a game. Win or lose, it doesn't matter. It quickly becomes clear who is impossible to beat and who is hardly worth the effort.

Slowly, just as I pictured it doing, my life and my game close up the big hole once filled by my father.

If I go to play chess straight from work, I get back to Isabelle's late in the night. She is always up, reading case histories or doing other job-related paperwork. If I have spent the day studying and come home for supper, I find her eating radishes or sardines from a little tin. Sometimes she goes to an exercise class after work. Or a concert. Normally, she will just stay home, working and drinking endless cups of hot water.

She has a number of friends, but they all have children. I

hear her on the phone asking after little Petra, Lilli, or David. I understand that the way in which Isabelle is alone is not pleasant for her. I am annoyed at not having grasped sooner that when I moved out of Mr. Aldrich's apartment I was not the only one to be banished by the daughter's arrival.

I'd like to tell Isabelle about all the things that loneliness, if handled properly, can produce. Solitude and quiet. Time to fill as you see fit. You become filled with ideas and patterns that choose *you* because you are available. You can sit alone with clean, empty spaces that are waiting to hold the new ideas, the different patterns.

Instead, I arrange to play an exhibition at the club and invite her. I know that Stas said no to exhibitions, but this is not for money. And, anyway, where is he, I'd like to know.

The club manager is thrilled. He has been asking for an exhibition since the day my father left me here. Isabelle, even more than I had hoped, loves the place. She often drops by in the evenings, stopping at home first to shower and change. She watches games in progress and flips through books. If interested, Isabelle is a good listener, and rare is the grandmaster who can resist telling how he got out of an impossible position with a brilliant combination. She listens. She reads. She drinks hot water from a Thermos. She is careful never to disturb me.

Five

MY GRANDFATHER READ A LOT. THERE ARE BOOKS ABOUT COUNTRIES, about wars and about governments. There are novels by three different British writers, one of whom I recognize by name from Mama's shelves. There are books on chess and books on theater history. Art history books. There are biographies—some about presidents and prime ministers, others about the writers whose novels are lying here in great heaps.

It takes until I have unpacked all twenty-three boxes for me to realize that it makes no sense to divide the books into only fiction and nonfiction. I try to make four major groups: history, fiction, chess, and biography. By now all of Clarence's sitting room floor as well as his tables—end, coffee, and dinner—are covered by my haphazard piles.

When I began, I put all the books about Africa in one place, not guessing that they belonged in both history and biography. There are five books on Algeria, and I had to look at a map to find out where it is. It is a country in Africa, *not* the city in Egypt where the library burned down.

The city I thought was Algeria is Alexandria. I have no idea why I know anything about the fire, the library, or the city itself. It's one of many things that slipped into my mind while I was thinking of my feet.

I am the walking definition of ignorant. Or my grandfather read too much. Either one could be the case. I can take my pick.

My favorites are the chess books, of which there are

forty-seven, neatly spread over my father's blue velvet couch. All of them have black-and-white checkered diagrams with incomprehensible captions like **3. Bh4 g5 4. Bg3 f4 5. e3 h5.** Some of the books are in Hungarian and are not to be confused with the many in French.

"He liked to play," Clarence says when I ask about these particular forty-seven. "When we were posted in Hungary, Alexander had a counterpart whose son was a grandmaster. The boy gave us lessons."

A what-master? A boy gave my father and grandfather chess lessons? They couldn't find a grownup? We are on the terrace outside the sitting room, peering into the crowded apartment. We have agreed that I need to pack the books back up.

"I'll never remember all the titles," I say. "It will be twenty-five or thirty years before I have any time free for reading."

"You'll want to make a catalogue," Clarence says.

A brief and unpleasant vision of the libraries I have waited in for Mama throws itself into my thoughts. Off-white, white, and yellow cards trapped in long, narrow drawers. The tyranny of the alphabet. A type of order and discipline that does not result in a performance.

"Good God, Phebe," he says. "From the look on your face, anyone would think I was sending you into a Latin American prison."

"I'll get everything cleared away," I say. "By tomorrow night, we can go inside."

"I have a young friend," Clarence says. "I'll see if he is up to the task."

"To make a catalogue?" I ask. "Or to put them away?"

"Both," he says, his smile thin but amused.

"Okay," I say, certain that in this moment my father reminds me of no one so much as myself. The look I see on his face is the one I get when I manage to change a difficult combination of steps from instructions into dance. I hadn't known I shared any expressions with my father, and I wonder why I see this one in him now. I try to puzzle it out but lose the whole thought as I sort my tights, searching for one clean pair.

I see that it is less a job offer than a favor request, although he is going to pay me more than I am making at the hotel kitchen.

"I don't think she's very bookish," Mr. Aldrich says. "Only we don't want to create the impression that I think that."

"I don't have to make any impression at all," I tell him. "I can make a catalogue while she is taking class."

He has told me that she is here due to some difficulty with her dancing. That she is a dancer. I have refrained from asking why anyone would be a dancer. What on earth does it mean? Why not be a clown? Who would deliberately train so as to perform for others? Horrible.

"You should *help* her to make the catalogue," Mr. Aldrich says. "They are her books. She needs a project. Her mother asked me to get her involved in something."

"Something other than dance class?" I don't pretend to know what dancers do, but I'm guessing they don't become involved in things other than dance.

"Yes," he says. "It's advice Phebe's mother says the dance school gave."

I have seen posters for ballet performances. Both at home and in London. The ones in London had pictures of girls who looked like creatures from another world. I hope his daughter just looks like a regular girl. That in itself will be difficult enough.

"Come for dinner tonight," he says. "We'll get everything started."

I am, of course, supposed to meet Isabelle tonight. At the club. It's not an official plan, but I would want to alert her if I wasn't going to be there. Which would involve telling her that I was expected at Mr. Aldrich's. To meet the daughter. An invitation Isabelle herself has not received.

I have an awful track record when it comes to handling divided loyalties. Mr. Aldrich, of all people, should know this. He is normally more considerate. I decide to spell it out for him.

"I think it will hurt her feelings," I say. "I mean, if I am at dinner and she isn't."

"Phebe will be there," he says. "I want you to meet each other. That's the whole reason for coming."

"Not your daughter's feelings," I say. "Isabelle's."

Mr. Aldrich sighs, turning his head from me to his office window, which overlooks the corner of Rue Gautier and Quai Wilson.

"I am twenty-two years older than Isabelle," he says. "It's not just for my own sake that I have left her in peace for a few weeks."

I absorb what he is saying. I think of how to answer by trying to hear it as Isabelle would. She already knows how old he is. She likes him enough to have let me move in to her living room. Enough not to have met anyone else during the year in which they have been friends.

"Of course you know best," I say, "but I have the distinct impression that she has not found it very peaceful."

"Come to dinner tonight, Nikolai," he says, turning back to face me. "I will speak to Isabelle myself regarding your whereabouts."

Without him, I would be back in London with an expired visa. There was never any doubt as to what I would do tonight. When I leave here, I won't return to the club, but to Isabelle's apartment. I have to wash out my other shirt and steam my suit.

While Mr. Aldrich clears the table and prepares dinner, the daughter and I take a cursory look through the books, which she thinks fall into four sections. I see almost immediately that the books are a map of her grandfather's diplomatic career. There are books on the history of each country to which he was posted. Books on artists from each country. Books by political and military leaders in the two World Wars. The fiction is, for the most part, by Western writers preoccupied with Communism. I avoid explaining any of this, hoping that it will slowly become clear.

"We'll need index cards," I say. "One for each book. Your father has some in the little room."

"Does he?" She asks this with a slight incline of her head. Her body is full of energy and ideas. Her movements precise and graceful. There is a crackle in the air around her. It is all very alarming.

"Yes," I say. "With his stationery and old calendars."

Once in the small room between the bedrooms, I can't find a thing. She stands in the doorway.

"Why would he keep old calendars?" she asks.

"I don't know," I say. "I must have been mistaken."

"My father told me you're a chess champion," she says. "Do they make mistakes?"

Her eyes are gray. I suppose they would be lovely if they weren't staring at me and surrounded by so much mascara. Isabelle wears it too. Whenever I see a tube of it in her bathroom, it makes my eyes itch.

"They do," I say. "It's often the only way to win. By someone else's mistake."

"Yes, I can believe that," she says. "I've always looked at a dancer's injury as a present to the rest of us."

I close the drawer I have been searching through, turn, and stand as tall as I can. Without my habitual slouch, we are the same height. I watch as we take a measure of each other. This is how I look at someone during a match. I see that she already knows me better than her father does. That we both have spent a lot of our lives anticipating the failure that comes hand in hand with winning. A slow, warning pressure starts along the right side of my neck.

I get through dinner by trying to sit up straight. Phebe has very good posture. Beautiful table manners. They are almost ridiculous in that you cannot help but notice them. Which makes me think of how awful mine are. Not as bad as those of my father, who used his knife as a second fork and did not concern himself with chewing quietly. Or with his mouth closed. I am careful to put my fork down between bites and to keep my elbows off the table. I answer questions sparingly, eyeing the piles of books surrounding us.

Dessert, a small chocolate cake with cream frosting, is set out on the table. Mr. Aldrich has a second glass of wine and Phebe refills the water pitcher. No one offers to slice the cake. Phebe looks at it in silence.

"Nikolai, would you like some cake?" Mr. Aldrich asks after an interval of time.

"My mother and I just look at dessert," Phebe says. "Isn't that odd?"

"I have thrown out more cake recently," Mr. Aldrich says, cutting the cake and putting half of it on a plate for me. "Cookies. Strudel. Pastry."

"It's a bad habit," Phebe says.

"You don't like sweets?" I ask her, picking up the small dessert fork from the top of my place setting.

"I don't like to eat them," she says.

Somehow the meal is finished. I drink a lot of the water, feeling the sure, fiery spread of my headache. Phebe asks if I would mind playing once with her father before I go. She has become quite curious about the game from the books.

"They are wonderful books," I say. "They would interest anyone."

"So you've read them?"

"Yes," I say. "Some helped me while I was in Zurich."

"You took them to Zurich?" Phebe says. "I didn't know they had traveled."

"Nikolai has a powerful memory," Mr. Aldrich says. "I thought he might add some of Alexander's collection to it."

"You mean you memorized them?" Phebe asks, walking over to the couch where she has placed them. "All these diagrams and numbers?"

"The useful ones," I say, watching her father set up his small, perfect chess set.

The bones under my eyebrows are aflame, but I have played entire tournaments in worse shape. Mr. Aldrich is a strong amateur player and I usually hold back, letting him fall into trouble instead of creating it myself. But tonight I have him in check within eighteen moves. In three more it will be mate unless he can figure out how to make his bishop work. He can't see what I can, but he can see enough, tipping his king over.

"Thank you, Nikolai," he says.

Phebe is quiet as they drive me home, but she gets out of the car to shake my hand, smile, and say she looks forward to tomorrow. We have agreed that I will meet her at the studio before we go to her father's apartment to impose order on her grandfather's books. Mr. Aldrich has an appointment preventing him from joining us. I smile back at Phebe and thank them both again for a lovely meal.

When I go inside, Isabelle looks up from her desk, her papers spread out.

"You're white as a sheet," she says.

I nod and pitch down onto the floor. I loosen my tie and roll over onto my back.

"It's only as bad as it looks," I tell her, pressing the freezing cold towel she gives me over my eyes.

"I know," she says, laughing, but softly. Noise is a horrendous problem during one of these episodes. In a moment she slips another towel around my neck. "Clarence called this afternoon. Thank you, Nikolai."

After a bit she brings me a square red pill. I know that it will erase the pain, but will also cause a light sleep full of vivid, hideous images. I swallow the pill and spend the night pressing ice against my head. When asleep, I dream of chess pieces shaped as creatures that seem to be swans crossbred with young girls. As a result, they look much the same as a grown-up, elegant woman. How can this be? my dreaming self asks, but it is. Each of the creatures moves according to the rules that govern a rook and each wears a shawl and, improbably, a silver bracelet. When I wake up, it is with neither chess nor blankness, just an absence of pain.

I think, not for the first time, that I miss my mother more than can be normal. I think, not for the last time, that some-day I will let myself look for her.

SIX

THERE ARE INDEX CARDS IN THE TOP DRAWER OF THE TABLE
between the beds in my room. I remember having seen them,
briefly, when I filled that drawer with bobby pins and elastics.
Some had writing in an odd arrangement of letters and numbers, which I now know concerns chess. It is more than likely
that I am looking at Nikolai's handwriting.

So he lived here. How recently? Odd how my father didn't
mention it. Nikolai, no doubt, packed up as soon as Clarence
got the call. The one saying I needed to arrive. I wonder what
kind of trouble Nikolai is in. What does he need from my father? That he needs something, I do not question.

Mama says that in addition to being a constitutional
bachelor, Clarence is committed to changing the world.
Slowly and the hard way: one person at a time.

"He means well," she told me once. "And he's often very
successful in his efforts. It's just so . . . correct."

I used to think, as much as I ever thought about it, that
Mama meant there was a coldness in my father's efficiency
that she could not—would not—find appealing. Now I don't
know what she meant.

There was such a contrast in their faces—my father's and
Nikolai's—tonight. I watched them as their game unfolded.
Clarence was consumed in what he was doing. He was alert,
wary, and peaceful. I have never seen him look like this.
Nikolai was a thousand miles away as he moved his pieces.
Although each piece moves differently, his all looked as if
they were working with the same choreographer.

I thought of fire and ice as I watched them, but who was which changed from moment to moment. What was very clear to me was that this boy fit with Clarence in a way I never have.

I have enjoyed our visits over the years, but that's all. They've not been necessary, no matter what the experts say about father figures. I think it is safe to say that Clarence and I are not crucial to each other. If I had to choose between my parents, there would be no contest.

Clarence is important to Nikolai. I don't know why, but I could see it during dinner. I'm sure there's more I don't know. Much more. My father has the right to matter to someone. I'll never find out from that strange, quiet boy what he needs.

I pick up the cards and put on my bathrobe. Clarence is still up. He has trouble sleeping and likes to sit on the front terrace, watching the darkness obliterate his mountain view.

I sit down in the empty chair next to him and hand over the cards.

"He left these in my room," I say.

"I should have told you," Clarence says, not even looking down, just holding the little pile with care. "I didn't know where to start."

"He needs help?" I ask, thinking that is as good a place as any.

"Who doesn't?"

Who indeed. I try again. "What kind of help?"

"There's the easy stuff," Clarence says. "Money, shelter, visas."

Sitting here on the balcony wrapped in my robe, next to a man I know little about, looking into the darkness, I have a creepy glimpse of my life years from now. An equally creepy glimpse of what it was like for my mother to be here some fifteen years ago. Will I also sleep with men I don't intend to love? If so, why? What will it feel like? With these questions in mind, I believe Clarence when he says money, shelter, and visas are the easy stuff.

"And the hard stuff?" I ask, wanting to know.

It's not that I think I can help. Nikolai is a chess champion. His English, while excellent, is spoken with a quiet hesitation. He is thin in the way boys who don't know they have bodies, and therefore appetites, are. His eyes could be any color or size behind the glasses he wears. We have nothing in common, but I do understand that even if he doesn't take class, his life is chess in much the same way mine is, or was, ballet.

His face was pale when he played Clarence. His eyes remained hidden except for their brightness. Nikolai leaned over the board until he seemed to own it through sheer brute strength. An illusion, of course, but on good days I have seen similar transformations in my classroom mirror.

"The hard stuff is that he's looking for someone." Clarence takes hold of my hand. He still does this. When we sit outside at restaurants, walk through crowds, or cross the street. He doesn't seem to have ever noticed, as Mama did, that I am too big—too old—for this. "He's looking for someone who doesn't wish to be found."

"Who is it?"

"A chess player. One of many. But Nikolai thinks that only Stanislav Vlajnik can transform him into a grandmaster. A grandmaster of grace and beauty."

I assume a grandmaster is the chess equivalent of a soloist, and that one of grace and beauty is like a principal dancer. A slight step up, which brings new rewards but also its own set of problems.

"You can find him, right?" I ask. My father's entire job, his whole life, is about tracking people down and getting them what they need. He can take charge of any crisis. If you need help, if you are lost, Clarence is your man.

"Vlajnik is not a good person," he says. "He's not someone Nikolai needs to know well."

This is information, and I file it as such. It is not an answer.

"But you can find him," I say. "Right?"

"He's cyclical. Some months he plays brilliant chess. Some months he's unfit for civilized society."

"You can't find him?" I ask. "Not even when he's well?"

"I've consulted friends in the chess world," Clarence says. "Other grandmasters. They think Nikolai has been through too much to take up with a man like Vlajnik."

"Does Nikolai agree?" I ask, wondering why it matters what anyone other than Nikolai thinks.

"As far as he knows, I'm still looking," my father says and I let his words float into the night.

"What does he do in the meantime?" I ask, slipping my hand away from my father's. "While he waits for you to find his teacher, what is he to do?"

"You think I'm lying to him," Clarence says.

"I don't think you're telling the truth," I say. More seriously, I don't think he knows the truth, what's true for Nikolai about Stanislav Vlajnik as a teacher.

At the Academy, André teaches class three mornings a week during the summer intensive. He is a mean, unforgiving taskmaster. The speed and clarity he wants are always beyond what we can do. But by the end of my first intensive, I would have died for him, as it was clear that what he wanted most was to turn us into ballerinas.

Only you had to be in class to realize this, and even then a few girls quit. So if my father and his friends judge a man not fit for civilized society, it doesn't mean this same man isn't a perfect teacher.

"Here's the truth as I understand it," Clarence says.

He outlines, in careful language, how he came to meet Nikolai. Vlajnik had agreed to teach him, but on one condition: He had to get rid of his father. Nikolai's father, Clarence tells me, would put any stage mother to shame: an overbearing, controlling man who knew nothing of chess but ruled his son's studies and tournament schedule. In short, a bully.

Nikolai told Vlajnik that it would be almost impossible to escape his father. That he had tried to leave him before, to no avail. "*He* must leave *you*," Vlajnik said and told Nikolai how to proceed. He should find a way to lose in the first round of the Salzburg tournament and tell his father on whose orders he was acting. Then in Geneva, where he was booked for a simultaneous exhibition against high-ranking masters, Nikolai should move every single game to a draw.

Vlajnik told Nikolai that his father would keenly feel the disloyalty involved (not to mention the loss of income) and it would provoke him to leave. If for some reason it didn't, Vlajnik promised to arrive in Geneva anyway, ready to teach. All went according to plan, but Vlajnik failed to appear.

Nikolai waited for ten days before telling anyone he had no money, no father, no plan. Clarence was eventually phoned (a friend of his manages a chess club here), and arrangements for the easy stuff were soon set in motion. Ten days. Each day must have seemed more horrible and endless than the one before. I wonder how long I could have lasted waiting. Waiting all alone for my future to show up. I have a surge of admiration, fear, and curiosity. For Nikolai, his father, and Vlajnik.

"He's not a man I want to hand Nikolai over to," my father says.

"He asked you to look for him, though," I say. "He should at least know that you aren't."

"That's what Isabelle says."

Isabelle? I have met a few of my father's women friends. He has a type—blond, well groomed, very severe. He doesn't stay interested in any of them for long and says it's a waste of time for me to meet them. So, in fact, I have met only the ones who have insisted on an introduction.

"Who is Isabelle?" I ask.

"A friend of mine," Clarence says. "Nikolai is staying with her. She's become involved in his chess a bit. She thinks we should either track Vlajnik down or tell Nikolai that we won't."

"She's right," I say. "He should at least know what his options are."

There's no response. I try to make out my father's profile in the dark.

"It's late," Clarence says after a while.

Well, yes. It was late when I sat down. Eventually, I know,

I'll get to that point where boys are men and not such a threat to my life in ballet. I might wind up, once again, sitting next to a man I don't know late at night while wrapped in my robe. I hope it won't bother me as it does now—to have no bond at all with a man to whom I should be securely tied. I put my hand back out toward Clarence.

"May I speak to him about what you know?" I ask.

If I could help Nikolai, my father and I would have, just this once, something in common. That would be nice. Perhaps important.

"If you feel that you must," Clarence says. "Maybe it will sound better coming from a lovely young girl instead of an old man."

He reminds me to latch the terrace door. I stay up long past his going to bed. I don't think I have ever been less tired.

I ask if she might want to organize the books by country. We consider the four haphazard groups crammed into every corner of the room.

"Fine," she says. "How do we know what country the books are from?"

"Not according to *where* they're from," I say. "The books are *about* several different countries."

"Which ones?"

What is it that girls think about? Does she really need to ask me this? "Poland, Hungary, France, Algeria," I say, picking books up one at a time. "Great Britain and India."

There's Cuba, South Africa. Belgium and the Congo. The

countries created by war and colonialism. Can she not see this at all?

"I thought they were all about art and chess and dead men," she says.

"Yes," I say. "But they are also about different countries."

"Okay," she says. "It didn't seem like that to me."

"There are many different ways to organize them," I say. "Dead men and chess is broad. If we do it by country, we can make smaller piles."

"Okay," she says. "He read a lot."

"He traveled quite a bit for work," I say.

"I suppose," she says, gliding over to the far side of the couch. She stands before them with a graceful indifference.

I start at the table by the terrace door, making an index card for each book, trying to interest her in the topic of each. She is not interested and simply nods at my summaries. I have made thirty-four cards when she asks if I want something to drink.

"Thank you, no," I say.

"Do you mind if we take a break?" she asks.

"Certainly," I say, looking up from my pen. "Are you unwell? Do you need something to drink?"

"No, I'm fine," she says. "It's only that I . . . well . . . I, I wanted to ask you a few things and you're very hard to talk to when you're working."

When I met her this afternoon outside her ballet class, she immediately bypassed my greeting with an incoherent apology about my room and how she'd had no idea. Once I sorted out what she was saying, I told her it was her home and that she needn't ever think of it. That I was fortunate even to know a man as kind and generous as her father. She asked where I lived now and I told her with friends.

I had rather hoped that was the end of her questions about my life. I'd like to tell her that she makes me tired. That she is too thin, too pulled up, too prepared. And for what? Her body is like her questions. A pounce. I'd like to say, Phebe, please sit while I impose order on this library in which you have no interest.

"Of course," I tell her, putting my wishes aside. "What did you want to ask?"

Her fingers fly up to her ears to rearrange hair that is already perfectly placed. I don't know if this habit of hers indicates that she is nervous or thinking.

"What happens if you don't find Vlajnik?" she asks.

Nothing good, I think.

"You mean Stas," I say, knowing that her question can mean only that she and Mr. Aldrich have discussed me at some length. It wasn't, then, a casual conversation about who used to stay in the guest room.

"Yes," she says. "If he's the only one who can help you, what would happen if he didn't?"

She really is making every effort to stay still, and as the air around her settles, I hear what she means her questions to convey. There is concern and a real apology.

"I don't know," I say. "Why?"

"No one has been looking for him," she says. "My father thinks Vlajnik abandoned you here."

During those ten days, I never felt abandoned so much as I knew I was lost.

"He has to have had a reason," I say. "It's why I have to find him. I thought your father understood that. I want to know what I did wrong. Stas wouldn't have asked me to go to so much trouble if he didn't mean to keep his word."

I stop talking, knowing I could go on for hours reviewing what I may or may not have done according to Stas's demands. This is already the most I have said on the topic to anyone.

"My father thinks Vlajnik isn't a well person," she says. "That he wouldn't be overly good to you."

"He plays as if all that matters is how he's playing," I tell her, forgetting that she has no way of knowing what that means. "It doesn't matter how he treats me."

"It matters to Clarence," she says. "It matters a great deal to him how you are treated."

"I still want to find him," I say. "I must find him. I mean nothing disrespectful, but your father is wrong."

"I think so too," she says. "But we'll need help convincing him. I mean, I don't think you can find Vlajnik without a grownup."

"My expenses are always small," I say, which is certainly true. If we'd lived on my idea of a budget instead of his, my father might have felt less impoverished.

"I wasn't thinking of money so much," Phebe says. "More of the unpleasant reality that you can't rent a car or even check into a hotel as a minor. Also, I'm sure your visa has all kinds of time and geography limits on it. We'd never get an embassy to deal with one of us."

She remains lost in thought, her fingers tapping on the table. I'll have to revise my original assessment of her mental capacity. She may not know much about books or world politics, but she knows what she needs to in order to confront obstacles.

"Do you think I could meet Isabelle?"

This is unexpected.

"I'm sure she'd like that very much," I say, choosing each word with care.

"I think she'd be willing to help you look," Phebe says. "Or at least be able to change Clarence's mind."

"I'll speak to her," I say, amazed that a day that had started so badly could end with my having a plan and an ally.

seven

As boys go, he's not that hard to be with. While Clarence and Isabelle negotiate the pros and cons of my meeting her, Nikolai and I spend a few days together. We make cards, or rather, he makes them and then I put the catalogued book back in a box. He is very persistent in his attempts to make me understand why and how the books are related to one another. I am persistent in not needing to know.

We go to his club, where he studies and I try very hard not get in anyone's way. I look forward to seeing his quiet, guarded face waiting for me after class outside of the studio.

I, of course, have made no friends there, and I know this is due to my own shortcomings. Mama says I am a little too self-absorbed to extend myself to others. She thinks it's a natural byproduct of becoming a performer.

"You are the star of your own universe." She says this whenever I have failed to do my homework or if I don't notice that a new girl at the Academy has, in fact, been there for a year. In my level.

Okay. Whatever. Maybe this is true. It might just be, as Nikolai thinks, that I am busy with other things.

"You go there to dance," he says. "If you wanted to make friends, you would go to summer camp."

He had never heard of summer camp before he and his father left home. At first, Nikolai couldn't understand why it existed. A place where your time is not your own and you *pay* to live with strangers with whom you have nothing in common? In the woods? The point?

When he learned that kids want to go and why (no parents, no work, fun, fun, fun!), it became one more thing he found seriously devoid of all appeal. Nikolai has some harsh views on ordinary things, but they all serve to support how his life is shaped. Anyway, who am I to pass judgment? It is not as if I am a stranger to harsh views on ordinary things.

I can tell he doesn't exactly approve of my goal in life, which is to end each evening taking a bow. But he likes that I have, as he says, removed myself from others to pursue what I want. We have both done this, and that is all we have in common. He probably would never willingly sit through a ballet, and I find chess as boring as homework.

The pieces all move according to their own rules and have different point values. The winner is the person who, finally, either checkmates the other king or winds up with more points on the board. Without a clock, a game can take forever. With a clock, each player has two and a half hours, which can feel like forever. Nikolai prefers to play on the clock, but not because it finishes sooner. The time used to play chess is, he says, time that stops the rest of the world.

I'd have to play in order to know what he means. Even when I stood at the barre with my mind firmly in my feet, I never thought the rest of the world stopped. I simply thought it was irrelevant.

Which is, I realize, how most people—regular people, not only regular girls—think of ballet. And chess. Chess is even more irrelevant to the world. I've never heard of chess having, say, a season or a gala opening or a star.

Clarence says this is because I live in America and don't

know the right papers and magazines to read. I always have to re-map my thoughts when my father refers to the country I live in as a foreign place. As another country lacking certain desirable traits. I know that it does, but I would never think so without his prompting.

"Chess is its own world," Clarence tells me. "This boy could run it. Watch him play."

I do. It is the only part of chess I find at all interesting. When Nikolai is sitting at the board playing someone (or playing himself, which is my favorite), you can tell from his body and his expressions that the most tremendous effort and thought and figuring are going into everything he does.

That the pieces demand so much from their player is something I like very much. I might like more if I could understand more, of course, but Nikolai won't give me lessons.

"I couldn't be a worse teacher," he says. "If I tried, I couldn't be more horrible."

The club's books are all in French. Or Russian. Very helpful. Among my grandfather's forty-seven books on chess, I find one published in England and called *Start Chess Right!* I wouldn't say that I can use it to teach myself, but I figure out a few things I find interesting.

Most professional players use seconds the way boxers use sparring partners. They use trainers to help them analyze moves and games. Seconds, therefore, tend to be young men and trainers, older ones. Like ballet, chess is at once a sport and a mind game. There are more than a few things about the mind game that I find incomprehensible.

"What is a draw?" I ask Nikolai.

"Neither side wins," he says. "There are different positional reasons for its happening, but a draw is a draw."

So he wasn't lying about being a terrible teacher. A draw is a draw, I think. Didn't Clarence say something about a draw when he told me how Vlajnik provoked Nikolai's father into leaving?

"How do you move a game to a draw?" I ask. I will never understand how you lose a game on purpose, and how you *win* one is beyond my brain's abilities.

"You plan and you make that your goal," Nikolai says. "I suppose your father told you about my exhibition here?"

"Yes," I say.

"I was surprised at how easy it was to draw each game," he says. "But then, I was up against people who couldn't see far enough into it."

"See what far enough?"

Nikolai looks among the books for Clarence's chess set. His hands move the pieces into a certain position. Of course, we aren't at the club. I would never talk to Nikolai while he was studying.

"It's white's turn to move," he says. "This could happen, resulting in this." He moves a rook and two pawns, and then a bishop takes a knight. "Or this." He moves a knight, a bishop, three pawns, and another bishop.

No pieces get taken. Nothing happens. He could be talking Russian for all that I can grasp of the point he thinks he is making.

"I can see moves and their results," he says. "That's what I do."

"Here's what I see," I tell him, moving all the pieces back to their starting position. "It's like a ballet company."

"No," he says. "I doubt it."

"The pawns all move in the same way, so they are the corps," I say, explaining. "The rook, bishop, and knight have smaller parts than the queen, but different from one another's. They are soloists. And the queen is the principal dancer."

"What does that make the king?" he asks.

Good question. What is the king in this game? It's the piece everyone wants to capture.

"The Brava," I say. "The point of the exercise. What you get for doing well."

"There are almost no women in chess," Nikolai says. "It would have to be Bravo."

"Why is that?" I ask. "Are women banned?"

There are no women in the club, and all the books I've seen are by men.

"I don't know," he says. "I think it must have to do with tradition. I have heard men say a lot of things about why women can't play. But I am unconvinced."

"Have you ever played against a girl?" I ask. "You know, a girl who can really play."

"Yes," he says. "There are these sisters who play beautifully. I won twice against the girl my age, but her younger sister is, I think, a stronger player."

"The younger one beat you?" I ask. That would be awful.

"Yes," he says. "With a little stuffed animal on her side of the table."

"Were you embarrassed?"

"No," he says. "I was impressed with her. She moved with great force. It was like playing a real army."

Huh. So much for my brilliant idea of how chess is like a ballet company. It is an army. Each game is a battle. Nikolai is always at war or preparing to wage one. And at sixteen, he is only a soldier. Maybe he will command the main army one day, as my father thinks, but just now Nikolai is looking for his general.

She is not as easy to bring to the club as Isabelle. I decide it's not Phebe's fault, exactly, but that she brings more of herself than is necessary into the room. The minute you look at her, you know more about her than you do about a stranger you might speak with at some length. In addition, she is curious about everything she sees. Isabelle is also curious, but she is less likely to launch into a barrage of questions.

Phebe wants to know a lot about Vlajnik. Did I play him? Yes. Did I lose or learn a lot? Both. Was he ever friends with my father? No. Did Vlajnik ever give my father a chance? A chance for what, I want to ask, but I will not supply an answer that gives away more than it hides.

"My father liked to keep me safely away from others," I say, picking up a book on Batista and a fresh card. I ask her if she knows that her grandfather was in Cuba during the two years before Castro came to power. It's hopeless. Her mind has raced on to another question. If I was kept so safely away, how did Vlajnik and I meet?

"People meet through their published games," I tell her. "Or at tournaments. It's how we know one another."

In truth, I didn't meet Vlajnik so much as he crept up on me. Slipped past my father's guard and spoke to me from the clean, graceful lines of his games. Games published only in Western magazines, which we read secretly, passing them on to one another with reluctance. You never read about him playing anywhere at home, but you'd know he'd won whenever only the second and third place winners were announced.

Vlajnik had crossed the government in some way, despite having been world champion once. Or maybe because of it. There were different rumors. For a number of years, he was barred from competitive chess. But he kept playing. Some of his most brilliant games aren't those he played in tournaments but those he played against himself when he was unable to face an opponent. The more my father forced me to study, the better I became and the more I understood what Vlajnik was up to.

When the authorities changed their minds and gave him permission not just to play but to travel, he resurfaced as a candidate for world champion challenger year after year. He never won, though, and I was sure I knew why. I studied his games and thought it was possible that he'd prefer to lose or draw than to win in an ugly manner.

This idea began to consume my chess hours. My father wanted to leave because he thought we could make more money in the West. I wanted to leave because I thought I could meet Vlajnik, beg him to show me how to live without winning. How to always let the pattern lead, whether to a win or a loss.

Nothing worked out exactly as my father or I planned. We did make more money, though. And I did, to a certain extent, learn how to let the patterns lead me.

* * *

At the club, the other members discern almost immediately that Phebe can't speak French. So in the middle of a game, my opponent might feel free to ask if she is my girlfriend. How far, if at all, have I gotten her to bed? Have I been, at long last, conquered by love? At first, I pretend I can't understand them. That my French doesn't cover sex and love or all that falls between these minefields of distraction. But my opponents are smart. And determined.

So they start mixing up their questions about Phebe with chess commentary. I can hardly respond to the one without the other. Trapped, I enjoy the fun they are having at my expense. The men have held to an unspoken code that my vanished father and no-show teacher are not to be discussed. In return, I have broken another code by bringing not one but two outsiders to observe them.

Among other things, I think they want me to know they prefer Isabelle's quiet, well-dressed presence to Phebe's energetic one. Who wouldn't make that choice? To the man who has asked if I am using my study hours in pursuit of carnal pleasures, I say, "She is in love with her toe shoes. We are not free to pursue such things."

"Where in America does she dance?" another man asks, pointing right to where she is standing.

Now she knows we're talking about her. No purpose in hiding it.

"They want to know where you go to ballet school," I tell her. "In America."

"The Academy of New York," she says. "On scholarship under André Rogovsky."

I tell the men. The one who pointed at her says, "She is a serious dancer, then. Rogovsky is famous for his ability to make talent work."

"Very serious," I say, hoping they will now give up on any ideas of my meaning anything to Phebe.

"A girl like that could break your heart," the man says.

No. Playing without ever finding Stas will break my heart.

"Nikolai would have to notice her first," my current opponent says. "Off the board the boy can't see a thing."

That's enough. I look far into the game currently under way. I protect my bishops. And when I am ready, I set them free to dominate the center, attack, and kill. It will be a long time before this man offers up a game or his opinion on my sight.

On the way back to Mr. Aldrich's apartment, Phebe is quiet. On other days, she has had questions about my games and those of the other players. I worry she is offended by having been a topic of conversation.

"The man you study with is very famous," I tell her. "Everyone was impressed."

"Of course. André will open a thousand doors," she says. "What did I do? Why were they talking about me?"

"You have an unusual appearance," I say, hoping *unusual* is the right word. "People want to know why."

"It's like being cursed," she says. "It's like working hard every day for the opportunity to be cursed."

"How do you mean, 'cursed'?"

"Looked at," she says. "Judged. Discussed."

"You don't like to be looked at?" I ask, thinking she has picked the wrong life.

"Not by men," she says. "Not like that. I am not a performance."

Surely there is a fine line between a dancer and her performance. Does she not see how she crosses this line many times a day? Many times an hour? Maybe a performance is not what I imagine. I should go to the ballet, I think, and am immediately alarmed. I should study. I should play well. I *might* go to the ballet. Why am I with this girl? Mr. Aldrich. Isabelle. Finding Stas. All good reasons.

"Your father has agreed for you to meet Isabelle," I say. "She told me this morning."

"Good," Phebe says. "I wasn't sure he'd come around."

"Isabelle says you have never wanted to meet the others."

"I've never been consulted," Phebe says. "He's so strange about his girlfriends."

"She says he didn't marry your mother," I say, surprised I have kept this information. Isabelle has spoken more than she can have meant to about Mr. Aldrich and his personal life. I thought I had carefully neglected to retain any of it.

"Correct," Phebe says. "My mother got a job in Berlin as soon as she found out she was pregnant."

It was Phebe's mother who didn't marry Mr. Aldrich. Not the other way around.

"Do you miss her?" I ask, actually interested.

"We talk on the phone every week," Phebe says. "I know I'll go home soon."

"Do you miss your father when you are home?"

"Not exactly," she says. "I wish I knew him better."

Her father is difficult to know in a way that I recognize as deliberate. I might tell her that even if she moved here she would find herself saying she wished to know him better. Except I could never help explain her father to her. I am good at chess, not at talking to girls.

It is while I am reviewing my skills and deficits that I realize the talking is helpful. I played really well today. The past few days. And I have studied with a huge blaze of clarity. It is helpful. To me, if not to her. She isn't easy to be around, but the extra energy she requires overflows into other areas. Of course I don't say this. Some things are best left in peace.

eIGHT

She looks just like Mama. Dark, curly hair. Thin without being skinny, and the same ski jump nose. Isabelle even dresses like my mother, in clothes that are stylish but not confining. She also, I cannot help observing, has perfect posture. Even as my desire to dance insists on fading, my happiness at seeing others use their bodies properly remains.

My father dresses well, but his shoulders round forward. Nikolai is a brilliant chess player, but he slouches. Isabelle is a stranger, but her posture puts me at ease. We are at a restaurant near Clarence's office. He thinks he is to meet Nikolai, Isabelle, and me here at seven. It is now six-thirty.

Nikolai and I arrived before Isabelle, and when she entered, he stood up and pulled out a chair for her. He had asked that a pot of hot water be brought to the table as soon as she came, and he has kept himself busy filling her cup and passing the bread. Around her, he has an extra layer of quiet reserve, so I doubt Isabelle has any idea that she is his focal point.

She and I have told each other how nice it is to meet the other one.

"You are even more lovely than your father had led me to expect," she says.

I'd like to tell her that she looks nothing like his other girlfriends. That I am completely unprepared to decipher what it means that she is a dead ringer for my mother. I settle on saying, "That's very kind of you."

"Phebe," Nikolai says, pointing to his wrist. He doesn't

wear a watch ("Ordinary time passes," he told me. "Why measure it?"), but he'd like me to get to the point.

"It's unlike Clarence to be late," Isabelle says.

"We told him you weren't free until seven," Nikolai says.

"Why," she says more than asks, her face quizzical.

"We want to find Stanislav Vlajnik," I say. "We will need help, and we hope you will agree to change Clarence's mind."

Nikolai and I have worked out what to say ahead of time. He wanted to ask her, but I reasoned that if she agreed and then Clarence became angry, she would blame whoever put her up to it. He said that in that case it should be me, but he thought I should make some changes to my wording. I had suggested saying, "We need you to change what Clarence believes is the truth." Nikolai said that, among other things, *the truth* sounded pompous and would make Isabelle dismiss us as self-aggrandizing young people.

"You mean as teenagers?" I had asked.

"I mean what I mean," he said. "Use my words. They're right."

"I don't know if I can change what Clarence thinks," Isabelle says to us now in a nondismissive way. "But I have wanted to talk with you about Vlajnik."

"Do you know where he is? You do? Do you? Where?" Nikolai asks, all his quiet reserve gone. "Have you talked to him?"

"No, no," she says. "He comes up in conversation all the time at the club. People can't believe how brilliantly you lost that game in Salzburg."

"I just did what he said," Nikolai says.

"You did more than that," Isabelle says.

"I lost," he says, looking down at his lap, "on purpose."

Isabelle turns to me. "Apparently, Nikolai used an opening or a variation or something that Vlajnik practically invented."

"He invented a way to lose?" I ask. "Aren't you supposed to win in chess?"

"That's the brilliance," Isabelle says, her eyes and smile sparkling like Mama's when she is about to tell me something new. "For Vlajnik, winning is a side benefit of playing beautiful chess, and so Nikolai found a way to lose beautifully."

"It wasn't that beautiful," he says to Isabelle.

"I've been told otherwise," she says.

"I made some deliberate, tactical errors in one of Stas's better openings," Nikolai says.

"He lost with brilliance," Isabelle says and, then, "Clarence is here. Let me bring it up."

My father and Isabelle kiss hello the way I have seen the girls at Mademoiselle's studio do. A murmured *bon jour* and a quick kiss on each side of the face. My father and Nikolai shake hands. Clarence kisses the top of my head while giving my shoulder a squeeze.

"All introductions done properly, then?" he asks, sitting down and unfolding his napkin. "Please forgive my delay."

He is, in actuality, ten minutes early. Mama, despite her well-documented talent for procrastination, has never been late in her life. She says any exposure to the foreign service will train you to prefer illness to tardiness. So I come by my punctuality honestly, from both sides. This is satisfying for reasons I cannot identify.

When did it start to matter what has come my way from my

father's side? If I am not turning myself back into one of André's dancers, what am I doing here? I used to follow changes in my life by keeping track of where and how my body was becoming stronger or more pliant. If change starts cropping up in my mind instead of in my body, how will I recognize it?

Now, stop, I say to my thoughts. We're at dinner to discuss Vlajnik, not for me to freak out at the possibility that I am like my father as well as like my mother. Clarence and Isabelle have a lengthy discussion about a change in policy at an organization where she used to work. When the food arrives (fish, vegetables, rice, sauce on everything), it is so good that I have to count bites.

"I have been talking with some gentlemen recently," Isabelle says. "Older, wiser men."

"Between your office and my company, how could you escape this fate?" Clarence asks.

"How, indeed?" she asks, and my father smiles at her.

They are flirting. Surely they are both way too old for this. Somewhere I have read (oh, God, please don't let it be one of Mama's articles, but already I know it is) that flirting is the language of sexual negotiation. Okay, this is fine, no big deal. We are here to find Nikolai's teacher. I can take whatever that will involve.

"These old, wise men are chess creatures," Isabelle says. "And they all tell me the same thing."

"I'm sure they do," Clarence says. "I hope you say you are already spoken for."

"Actually, they are not so interested in me," Isabelle says. "They tell me that you can't find Vlajnik because he's hiding. They think he's afraid of Nikolai and needs to be reassured."

My father says something in French. Vehemently and at some length.

"Nikolai's French is improving every day," Isabelle says, her voice steady, but barely.

"Not that much," Nikolai says. "I missed more than half."

There is a prolonged and fairly hideous lull in the conversation. Isabelle's hands rub the back of her neck, and the bracelets she has on jangle as they slip away from her wrists. Nikolai pushes his glass of water toward her.

"We don't know if he's hiding," I say finally. "All we know for sure is that he didn't show up when he said he would."

"We know other things," Clarence says. "He's mentally unstable. He could cause havoc in your game, Nikolai."

"No," Nikolai says. "That wouldn't appeal to him."

"He has a reputation for craving order," Isabelle says.

"I don't want to bring trouble," Nikolai says to my father. "But I need to see him. If only to ask what happened."

"We'd really like to find him," I say, so that Nikolai is not alone in asking for this. "A grownup has to help."

"Phebe, it's not as if I can place a few calls and produce him," Clarence says. "I have no idea of how to find a man who has no wish to be found."

"Of course you do," I say. "It's your job."

His job, his job. What on earth do I know about his job? That he is the European director for the Refugee Relief Committee is not all that illuminating. What does he do all day, and why did he retire early from the foreign service? Would I know these things if I had not spent the past six years locked up inside the Academy?

"The people I find have lost their countries and want my help," my father says. "Vlajnik doesn't want my help."

"But we do," I say. Can you help us? Will you?

"I have an idea," Nikolai says slowly, his face more guarded than usual.

Isabelle smiles at him, and he opens right up.

"I've done everything Stas told me to do," Nikolai says. "I think it might get his attention if I did something he has proscribed."

"Such as?"

"I'm not supposed to play for money," Nikolai says. "Or play in any simultaneous exhibitions. Perhaps I should start."

"Your father had arranged a lot of them," Clarence says. "I remember canceling them all over Europe."

"We could arrange them again," Nikolai says.

"It would involve a fair amount of traveling," my father says, looking at Isabelle.

"There's a big tournament in Venice," she says. "In August. All the chess creatures tell me Vlajnik will be invited."

"He is invited every year," Nikolai says. "He accepts only when he wants to."

"Phebe has class every day," Clarence says. "This trip will have to be yours and Isabelle's."

"You won't come with us?" Nikolai asks.

I understand very clearly, he is asking only my father to please help. Searching for Vlajnik without my father is not part of the plan. Regardless of Nikolai's plan or my own class schedule, I am not willing to sit out the search for Vlajnik. Or the attempt to get his attention. I want to know what a simultaneous exhibition is, and if you play chess for money, is it like gambling or getting paid to perform?

If I were at home, I would be well into the Academy's summer intensive. I would have neither the time nor the inclination to ask such questions. But I am here. In Geneva. Interested in the obsessive life of a boy in whom my father is interested.

Wait, I think, wait. If my father lives here, aren't I home? Or must I be near Mama in order to be home? I should find out. I should know what is important to me if class is no longer as vital as it was.

"I'll talk to Mademoiselle," I say. "There are other studios in other cities. She can help me make sure I stay in class."

I feel as if I have brokered a treaty between where my thoughts take me and what ballet demands. How clever.

"Are we planning to go to Venice, then?" Clarence asks. "Venice in the summer?"

"It's not an idyllic holiday," Isabelle says. "But we both have more than enough vacation time set aside."

"We cannot count on Venice," Nikolai says. "If people are telling Isabelle that Stas is hiding or afraid, then he won't be in Venice."

"You want to go to other places?" Clarence asks.

"Word should be spread that I am no longer waiting for him," Nikolai says. "No longer doing as he thinks best."

"You want to reschedule the exhibitions?" I ask. "The ones your father set up?"

"Yes."

"You hate playing them," Clarence says. "You've told me so."

"I hate playing while always wondering what Stas would advise," Nikolai says.

We are all silent. After all, no one likes to be haunted. Certainly no one likes to discover that someone at the dinner table is being haunted. Not by a dream or a ghost, in this case, but by an absence. So we will track Vlajnik down or lure him out. I will see for myself some of the places my father wanted to take me. The brochures, maps, and train schedules will be put to use.

PART TWO
OUT AND ABOUT, THEN

nine

WE'VE BEEN ALL OVER EUROPE, IN AND OUT OF AT LEAST TEN CHESS clubs, and we've changed money so many times I can no longer recognize a Swiss franc. No sight of Vlajnik in Amsterdam, Brussels, or Munich. The traveling is fun, but not conducive to a schedule, something Nikolai and I are united in needing.

I have to take class in the morning. Sometimes, if the class isn't great and I can't stay after to do my own barre, I have to return for another class later in the day. One taught by someone else. I have to negotiate all of this with people who let me know that their good English makes up for my inability to speak their language. I have to eat or not eat based on what classes I attend. And I have to find ways to be with Nikolai, my father, and Isabelle. After all, we've gone to a lot of trouble to set up these exhibitions, as well as the private investigations Clarence and Isabelle make.

Nikolai has to organize his sleep, meals, and studies around his exhibitions. He can't be tired or nervous or unprepared. He can't arrive in a strange city on the day of an exhibition. He needs a day or two to settle in to a new place and disappear into his game. On the days he doesn't have an exhibition, he has to study. Visit chess clubs. Find people who know people who know Vlajnik or his remaining friends.

Isabelle says that she has been told that there are only seven people in Vlajnik's inner circle, three of whom are insane.

"Only one," Nikolai tells us. "The other two pretend."

This is a strange world we are in. The men in it are young, old, and obsessed. They play chess all the time. Some of them have been playing one another for so long that they know exactly what move will meet theirs. They don't seem to be playing to win so much as playing for comfort. There are certainly those who play to win and find their solace in it.

Nikolai plays them all. He doesn't care. He cares only about playing. And, surrounded by these men who care just as much, he seems normal. We seem normal. Isabelle talks to everyone and is convinced that searching for a man as famously mysterious as Vlajnik is not only reasonable but imperative.

Vlajnik, who is "Stas" to the other players and "Vlajnik" to outsiders, was the world champion before either Nikolai or I was born. Vlajnik lost his title right back to the man he'd taken it from, who went on to keep it for six years before losing to the man who lost to the American who played once and then vanished, and so on. There are lots of ex–world champions. Vlajnik is one of the few who remain a consistent threat to the current two Kings, as Nikolai calls them.

Vlajnik was, after years of being refused, granted rare and generous travel privileges from the Kremlin, and he moved about Europe like a nomad. It was whispered that as a result he'd lost his title to a Good Soviet Citizen in exchange for freedom. Vlajnik lived briefly in New York and then San Francisco but decided that America was not a happy environment for chess. More whispering.

There's so much else I know about him and the world champions who came between him and the two Kings currently battling. But it's occurred to me that I don't want to know this much chess history. There appear to be about seventy-two people who know all that Nikolai knows, and their universe is farther away from life than ballet could ever be.

I'm glad that this other small world exists. I like that anyone with the right mixture of talent and dedication can find his or her place in this world. I like how important this world is to Nikolai. It is, however, impossible to ignore how very narrow and, well, limited this world is.

Until I stumbled into Nikolai's chess life, I had not known one could be so devoted to something unrelated to ballet. I had never seen how confining this devotion is. If I become a prima ballerina, that devotion will have set me free. But it may also, as I see from watching the devoted chess creatures, prevent me from having a life full of other interests.

What interests me, other than watching myself dance badly? I have to renew my vigilance. I must not become one of those girls who think too much to dance.

I decide that for now I will let my thoughts wander to chess and no farther. But not too far into it, or I will die of boredom. Nikolai himself *is* interesting, but only because he is obsessed. A lot of the men who talk to Isabelle and/or play against Nikolai call him Kolya. The name suits him, and I ask if I can use it as well.

"If you like," he says.

I do like, although I continue to think of him as Nikolai. I call him Kolya so as to join him in his world. From his world, I can see the flaws in mine more clearly. Nikolai can see what he must in this place where he is forced to win or lose. Each time he plays he must start all over.

I've tried to get him to talk about what it's like to win or lose a game. Some of the men I've watched him play against have been completely devastated at the end of a game, even when they've won. Nikolai says that grandmasters of a certain strength are horrified at how hard it is to beat him.

"They think it should be easier," he says. "So they judge themselves."

"How do you feel when it hasn't been so easy to win?" I ask.

"I prefer to win than to lose," he says.

That is the most he will say on the topic. *I prefer to win than to lose.*

Okay, then.

Isabelle says it's unhealthy for him to be too centered on his winning and losing. I personally don't see how he can live his life for chess without being totally preoccupied with victory and defeat.

"You have a good point," she says, and then, "Oh, I don't know. He should be in school. Is playing chess good for him?"

She thinks that Nikolai is brilliant. That he doesn't have to live a life built on such fragile concepts as *win* and *lose.*

"He could do anything," Isabelle says. "And while I respect that this is his choice, I worry about the kind of life he will have."

Now would be the time to tell her that she reminds me of my mother. But Isabelle's concerns about Nikolai's chess life probably mean she shares Mama's low opinion of the life I will have. Might have. Was meant to have. I am not exactly thriving in all the different atmospheres in which I am taking class.

I am still a good dancer. If I force myself, I have the necessary clean lines and the important strong balance. But I do have to force myself. Every time I pull on my tights, I cannot stop from asking myself, Is this worth it to you? Do you want this to be all that matters? Do you not see that the only difference between you and a chess creature or you and a regular girl is that you can bourrée across stage? Wow, you can walk on your toes.

I can remember what it took to get on pointe. But the joy and the triumph my body had are gone. I don't even need the mirror to see I am losing the fight to get my thoughts into my feet. This is the great and the horrible thing about ballet. If you are at all good, it is impossible to delude yourself into thinking you are better than you are.

"It's the same in chess," Nikolai told me.

In Munich, he asked me why I was so irritable at lunch. I told him partly because I was sick of eating in restaurants and partly because I was in the process of becoming a bad dancer.

"It's better to think what's true," he said, "even if it's a horrible fate."

"The truth can be a bit overrated," I told him, feeling more irritable than before.

I was glad he conceded that ballet might have something in common with chess. However, I doubted he would embrace the truth so much if it meant that he was becoming a bad player. This was not a point I felt compelled to make at the time. Perhaps after we have found Vlajnik, when the idea of playing badly seems more like a bad dream to him than a possible reality.

The only good thing about not finding Vlajnik is that I get to spend time with Isabelle. We share a sleeper compartment on the overnight trains, and when I am not with my father or in class, I am often with her. She is the first interesting grownup I have met who is not also a journalist. Isabelle is generous with her time and her things and her ideas of "unconditional support." She will do her best by Nikolai even though she is uncertain what is best. If he has to live with her until he is ready to move on, then all she has lost is her living room.

"In which I do precious little living," she says.

When I tell her that I think Nikolai is in love with her, she does not act alarmed or annoyed or dismissive. She says, "I think you are mistaking very good manners for something they are not." Which makes me have to rethink the situation. Whether he is or isn't, it's none of my business.

On the overnight train to Hamburg, Isabelle and I stay up late painting our toenails. Not very well, what with being on a train. I finally tell her that she doesn't look at all like the other women Clarence has dated.

"I am aware of this," she says. "I'll never know why he consented to have dinner with me. Perhaps he thought I wanted a job."

"You asked him?"

I thought girls took the initiative only in André's ballets. In André's ballets, the women not only have all the good parts, they have all the power. They pick the man they want to dance with and they leave when the music ends. I have noticed that this is not how life works. Not for regular girls.

"Clarence would never have asked me," Isabelle says. "He thinks he's too old for me."

"My mother is a lot younger than he is," I say, wanting her to know that age doesn't matter to my father. That she has nothing to worry about.

"Yes," she says. "Look how well that turned out."

Oh. I had never thought before of the accidental affair from Clarence's point of view. How it might not be so good to find out two years after the fact that you and your best friend's daughter have had a child. Oh. Or, rather, *Oh, my*, as Mama says whenever she doesn't know what to think.

Isabelle has never been married. Close a couple of times, but long ago.

"It's not on purpose," she says. "I don't think these things can be planned."

"What things?" I ask.

"You know, love. Husbands. Families. Children."

"I don't want children," I say, stopping myself just in time from explaining why.

André has said, repeatedly, that any woman can be a mother but not every woman can be a ballerina. Something tells me that now is not the time to pass on this bit of Academy wisdom.

"I don't want children either," Isabelle says. "But I don't want to be alone."

Nikolai has indicated that he thinks Isabelle is lonely. He gives as evidence that she stays up late working and drinking hot water. Whole lot he knows. The water is to keep her skin hydrated, and most women with jobs stay up late working. But perhaps my mother is also lonely. What do I think is behind those late nights with Scotch, which are not in any way work-related? Joy?

"My mother says Clarence is a constitutional bachelor," I say, hoping Isabelle has not been misled by anything my father has done or said.

"Believe me," Isabelle says, "your father was saying that before your mother was born."

"Doesn't that worry you?" I ask.

"No, it makes me think he knows himself."

"But if he's right, you'll be alone again."

She has finished with her toes. They gleam like the tips of a bronze statue. I am still working on mine with a more garish red, to clash with my very pink tights and shoes. My very pink life. Isabelle passes me the bag of cotton balls and what is left of the polish remover.

"Eventually, we will all be alone again," she says. "Right now I feel as if I'm not."

Without my having to ask about it, she has quelled my fears about more late nights wrapped in my robe, sitting next to a man I don't know. If I have these nights with men with whom I have no bond, I will be fine. More than fine. I'd still prefer to be tied to the men who are important to me, but either way I will thrive.

We do not find him, and he does not come looking for me. I play a lot of chess and I get through the exhibitions with minimal damage. I remember that it is important not to judge

myself as harshly during an exhibition as I would in a tournament. Or in a real game against worthy players. In Munich, I
had two games against a grandmaster, which were probably
the best in my life. I lost both, and losing is still as horrible as
ever, but my games were full of beautiful patterns.

No sign of Stas anywhere, although in Brussels Isabelle
found someone willing to admit he'd had dinner with Stas
less than a month ago and that when I came up in conversation Stas had allowed as how he hadn't done what he'd in-
tended. The man wouldn't tell her more except to say that we
should keep looking.

"A man like that is flattered by such attention," he said to
Isabelle.

When Mr. Aldrich heard that he said, "A man like Vlajnik
should be arrested."

"Then he'd be really useful to Kolya," Phebe said. "Let's
focus on the positive. Vlajnik had better, more honorable intentions. He just needs to follow up on them."

Phebe calls me Kolya. Isabelle sits down with men who
have devoted their lives to avoiding women and maneuvers
them into giving her their attention. Phebe and Isabelle
share a sleeper compartment on overnight trains because it is
simply too expensive to book three. It is easy to see they have
become friends. They are very different, but they stay connected in my mind.

Any feelings I might have for Phebe that could become . . .
complicated, I transfer to Isabelle. I know I have allowed myself to *fall* a little in love with Isabelle because of the impossi-
bility that surrounds *being* in love with her. In this way, I can
keep Phebe from becoming a problem while also knowing the

details of what passes for my ability to express love and desire. Eventually there will be room for all of these things. But until I find Stas, until my game has arrived at its first peak, I have neither time nor energy for girls or women.

For many years, I could coast on talent and studying. Somewhere between twelve and thirteen, I sensed that my desire to play was giving ground to something else. It didn't take long to guess what. My father thought he should take me to a prostitute, but I managed to evade this plan. I had no objections to his idea or his invasion of my privacy. I simply thought it would make a manageable problem worse. I have managed it and will continue to do so.

In London, I was overwhelmed by the pictures of women in magazines and advertisements who existed for pleasure. There was the wife of our landlord, who was less elegant than Isabelle, but as lovely. I have always found a place to lock up my sex life. I admire Phebe, but I would rather spend the night with Isabelle. If this is a trick my mind plays for the sake of my game, it is a trick that works.

Surely Stas will emerge to find out why I am letting myself play for money as if I were in the circus. I study and I search out games with men who might know my teacher. I play and I study in the hopes that if we lure him out, I will be prepared.

I have always liked travel. The people in a hurry at stations, in airports, on new and different streets. The business of finding places to sleep and eat. The way routine is won instead of granted. I think that the travel one does in order to play is a reward for the hours, the days, the months, spent alone in concentrated study. Travel is a legitimate distraction. Playing new people is thrilling in a way that shocks my mind and soothes it at the same time.

In the chess clubs we attend, I see a lot of familiar faces. Grandmasters who have watched my game for years. Boys I have beaten. Men known to work with the two Kings. Men who I know have lost many, many times to Stas. I play and I study and I enjoy being near the people who are, in some sense, my family. In Amsterdam, we run into the man I lost to last year in Salzburg. Jasper Greene. Jasper has a clean, sharp game. He can think fast and analyze with nuance. He is always in demand as a chess teacher when he is not playing to improve his own ranking.

I first met him when I was eight and he was nineteen. It was in Budapest. Jasper was part of the American team, which had been allowed to come and watch the junior champion tournament. Despite all the attempts to keep the Americans away from us, Jasper found a way to go over my games with me. My father, of course, accused him of trying to steal my ideas. I didn't see Jasper again until we arrived in London.

Jasper's parents are rich people who have tried everything to get their son to stop playing. He says he has been disinherited too many times to count. He went to a university in the States, but left after a year. He had to play chess more than he had to study. So he is here in Amsterdam, teaching and preparing for Venice.

I am absurdly happy to see him and make introductions to Mr. Aldrich, Phebe, and Isabelle. Phebe has just finished her morning class and is flushed with impatience and determination. The more frustrated she is with her class performance, the more her body presents itself as an object that demands something other than a passing glance. When she shakes Jasper's hand, I can almost see her curtsey.

Jasper ignores it all. He is quite good, although not perfect, at blocking out anyone of whom he doesn't have to be aware.

"You must come to Venice," Jasper says. "You will never find Stas otherwise."

"Are you certain he will be in Venice?" Isabelle asks.

"Who can say?" Jasper asks. "The only thing one can know of Stas is that one never knows."

"We'll keep looking until we do know," Mr. Aldrich says. He is still uncertain about Stas's ability to harm me, but he is willing to hunt for what I say I need.

I ask Jasper if he is free to play. If he will come back for the exhibition I must suffer through the next day.

"Of course," he says. "I should like to play when you are not so determined to lose."

And he vanishes. When he reappears, the day after my exhibition, we play to a draw three times.

"You make questionable choices," he says.

"I understand them," I say. "To me they are not questionable."

"Come to Venice, Kolya," Jasper says. "I will put you to work. Even if you find Stas, do come."

"If I find Stas, he will be the one to put me to work."

"Well, he's better than your father."

I have to wonder what makes Jasper think that my father, who never asked me to stop playing, was so terrible. It is widely known that Jasper's game suffers from his lack of discipline. That he is vulnerable on the board based on what is happening off of it. Can Jasper not see that his own father might have caused some of his shortcomings? No matter. He has forced me to play in a rigorous and beautiful manner. I hope I see him again soon.

On the night trains, I share a private compartment with Mr. Aldrich. He reads until almost four every morning. I wonder why he has so much trouble sleeping. In the hotels, I have my own room. It's rather nice to spread my books out and not be aware of anyone else's habits. At Isabelle's apartment, I sleep in an open space. These hotel rooms are more like the room I had when I lived at Mr. Aldrich's. Phebe's room.

Phebe is not as happy as I am in her own rooms in these strange places. She often comes to my room at night. All the hotel noises (creaky elevators, music from the bar, etc.) keep her awake. She rarely talks except to say how her class went. Beyond that, she mostly stands quietly, far from the surface I am using to work, and watches. This is, she says, as good as talking.

"I can practically hear you thinking," she tells me. "I don't understand any of it, but it's kind of like listening in on a private conversation."

I still haven't told her she brings quite a lot to my studies. I like how I am secretly taking the clear energy she carries everywhere. She seems completely unaware of it. If I were to bring it to her attention, I'm sure she'd be willing to share.

ten

WE KEEP GOING PLACES, NIKOLAI KEEPS PLAYING, AND VLAJNIK keeps hiding. My father makes arrangements for Venice. It would appear that Nikolai is not getting Vlajnik's attention by playing for money. Not yet. My father is willing to keep going.

"But if he's not in Venice, we will have to give it up," he says.

We will go home from Hamburg, do laundry, regroup, and then depart. Again.

"Stas is somewhere near," Nikolai says. "I'm sure of it."

Everyone Isabelle speaks to says Vlajnik is around. And full of regret about his behavior.

"Regret is not an emotion that spurs one into action," my father says.

He says this definitively, as if he were the final authority on regret. Perhaps he believes he is. Perhaps he thinks one needs to be a certain age to know about sorrow or doubt.

It is easier for me to observe Clarence during our travels. He seems more like a person to me than a man perpetually stuck inside his own ideas of what a father is. For example, he is horrified to discover I don't know what language is spoken in either Amsterdam or Brussels. I have some vague ideas about Flemish instead of the clear facts of Dutch and French.

"Good God," he says. "Not knowing one is excusable, but two is beyond the pale."

An opinion he would certainly have kept to himself while visiting in New York and probably, also, while I was visiting him in Geneva. Out and about, as we are, he buys a copy of the

Herald Tribune every morning, asking me to familiarize my-self with its contents.

"You mean read it?" I ask.

It's not that I've never read a paper before. When Mama worked for the wire service, her articles were in countless newspapers. It was a point of pride for me that I already "knew" what was in the paper. Only I didn't. I had simply watched her type or heard her on the phone trying to verify a source.

"I mean read it and learn what the world is doing," my father says, handing me a neatly folded *Herald Tribune*.

The print is really tiny, but most of the articles are short. The paper is thin, with its own peculiar smell—a mix of ciga-rettes and something clean. It is full of stories about parlia-ments and rebel forces and terrorists and floods. There are reviews of concerts and dance companies. A full page of comics. Two pages of columns and editorials. I skip those. Clarence usually circles two articles he thinks I should focus on, and we talk about them at dinner.

I now know a fair amount about a military coup and the economic consequences of natural disasters. Although the news is almost always bad, confusing, and upsetting, it is comforting to have consistent dispatches from the larger world. If my thoughts are so determined to venture outside of class, perhaps they should know what is out there. Mama will be both pleased and amazed. Isabelle is less ecstatic about my coerced reading schedule.

"You don't have to do it," she says. "It's possible to be well informed without knowing the native language spoken in each foreign city."

"It's not a viable possibility for the granddaughter of

Alexander Knight," Clarence says. "He would be turning in his grave."

I don't point out that he was cremated, which would make any kind of turning really hard. I read the paper. I watch my father check in to hotels and find places for us to eat. I go with him when he is hunting for Vlajnik in places other than chess clubs. Since Vlajnik doesn't play for money, the trail he makes winds through worlds apart from chess. My father examines Vlajnik's jobs.

When not playing chess, Nikolai's teacher works as an accountant. He does something called outside auditing, but because he doesn't like to work too many days in a row, he only agrees to audit the books on small businesses. Clarence is well connected with local government officials (or knows people who are). He can easily figure out which small hotels, cafés, and grocers (all favored by Vlajnik as employers) have turned in financial records.

Clarence is a good mix of polite and charming. I can tell this even when he is not speaking English. How people behave is a lot clearer to me if I can't understand what they are saying.

Aside from the jobs, Vlajnik seems to have had a number of wealthy friends, people who liked him well enough to have let him stay in their homes for extended periods. Or to have given him gifts. Always, the same thing seems to have happened. For no discernible reason, Vlajnik became enraged or offended and broke off the friendship.

My father is able to listen to a version of this story many times over and act each time as if he is hearing it afresh. He is careful to make the wronged friend's grievance a priority while also pressing for information about Vlajnik's current whereabouts.

After we have tea with the owner of a posh leather goods store in Brussels, I ask Clarence if he has always been so good with people. Or if he had to learn, the way I am trying to learn what is going on in the world. The world out here in life.

"I am not good with people," Clarence says.

"Yes, you are," I say. "No one has refused to help or been rude."

"I know how to get things done," he says.

"Well, isn't that the same as being good with people?"

"Not to my way of thinking," he says.

Okay, then. Fine. I know my way of thinking doesn't carry much weight.

"Your mother has a wonderful way with people," Clarence says. "She can make anyone believe he is the center of her attention."

He. Is that what happened? Did he think during the course of their accidental affair that he had all of Mama's attention? Was he, therefore, shocked when she left? Angry? My mother has always claimed that Clarence was relieved when she packed her bags.

"We knew it wasn't meant to be," she has said. "As such, it had already lasted too long."

I know very little about what happened, other than the facts Mama has told me. Certain facts that do not vary in the way her feelings do.

Mama's mother had recently died. It was a long illness, and Mama had quit her job at a newspaper in Philadelphia to take care of doctor visits, oxygen tanks, and at-home nurses. My grandfather had no talent for this kind of thing. My uncles were busy with their own families. With being *very married*. Mama, unmarried, looked after her mother as she died. Once or twice a month Clarence placed a call to Mama.

"I'm only phoning to say hello," he'd tell her. "How are things?"

Clarence had recently resigned from the foreign service. He had a new job in Geneva. After Mama's mother died, he invited Mama to spend Christmas with him. He had remembered her saying that the mere idea of the holiday season was unbelievably brutal.

So he invited her to Switzerland. She accepted gratefully. They had a good holiday. She stayed on for a while. And things happened.

"She is pretty good with people," I say. "You are too, but it's different."

"I am a fairly closed person, Phebe," he says. "I hope not so much with you."

"I think you are as open as you need to be," I say.

He takes my hand.

"Isabelle reminds me of Mama," I say. "The way she makes everyone feel like she is only interested in them."

"Perhaps," he says. "I had not thought of them as having much in common."

Really? Is he blind? Or is he, as he says, closed to certain obvious things?

"Are you going to marry her?"

"I would know such a thing as that," Clarence says, "only well after the fact."

This is the father I have met and known since I was three. The person who is hard to observe. As hard to know as he is capable of getting many, many things done. Luckily for me, this one walks hand in hand with the other father. The one whom I have started to know during our visits to distant cities.

I like him. We are similar in ways I cannot yet articulate. Perhaps I can still say that we are not crucial to each other, but I would never want to choose between him and Mama. Walking beside him down strange streets, I feel as if Clarence is one of my parents, not merely an old friend of the family who happens to visit on a regular schedule.

We will have to resort to Venice, after all. My idea has failed. There is no sign of or word from Vlajnik, and thus no progress off the board. On the board, something has happened. There's a flow that at first I fear is reckless. I have a thought and I make a move. Over the years, the time between the two (thinking and moving) has naturally reduced, except when preparation gives way to real life and I am confronted with someone's unexpected mistake or glorious idea. Then I have to stop, look, and calculate. The flow I've noticed seems to come from my brain's new ability to think without my noticing. It's as if chess itself is dictating what my hands do.

We are in Hamburg when this happens for the first time. During the club-sponsored exhibition, Isabelle is approached by several men requesting to play me the next day. I play two older men (one of whom is blind and has to be told my moves before announcing his) and win. Then a younger man, probably not much more than five years my senior. He favors an aggressive attack style that I have long disliked, but before I know it I am in a position to win.

As my hand reaches for a pawn on f3, I pull my mind back with an almost violent effort. The board is hideous. My pieces are working in combinations that look isolated, and as I try to recreate how they got to their current positions, I don't see beautiful patterns. Just mayhem. But I have material advantage, and I can sense my opponent weakening. He's a strong player, so there's nothing obvious. Still, I know if I keep it up, I'll win. But like this?

I have enjoyed the energy of playing in an unfamiliar style without a lot of self-critique or analysis, but I really don't know what to do here. If I let my thoughts go, I'll win. It's ugly. It's a win. I need someone I trust to tell me which is a better measure of progress.

My father never let me entertain these questions. Surely, Stas would. I look at the man opposite me. He thinks I've paused from fear, so I let the flow push me to a victory I can't approve of or enjoy.

That night, after dinner, there is a knock on my door. I put down my notes and let Phebe in. She slinks to a corner away from my books and the board I put out for show but never need. I see more clearly when I picture the board in my mind, but Stas prefers to use the board itself.

"I was better today," she says.

This is new. Most nights she claims to have been terrible in her morning class. It didn't matter to me one way or another until we were in Munich and Mr. Aldrich took us all to a performance by a touring Canadian ballet company.

It's all amazing. The way the music fills up the stage as if it were also a performer. The way the girls are brighter than the stage lights. The way they gain height by going up on their toes. The flying. The spinning. That music can move. It explains a lot about Phebe's overly mannered way of moving out here in life.

So now if she says she's better instead of terrible, I know that what she means is that she might have her chance, after all, to turn herself into light and music. And that matters. Not because she's been nice to me and Isabelle, who says she wishes Mr. Aldrich liked her as much as Phebe does. It matters because I have seen for myself why anyone with the chance to be a part of the ballet should never lose it.

"I'm glad," I say. "Was it the teacher?"

"Isabelle and I have been taking chess lessons from Clarence," she says.

"I know, I meant the dance teacher."

They asked me for lessons, but other than explaining the rules I really don't know how to teach. I know only how to work things out on my own, something I should be doing right now. Like analyzing my ugly win. I learned something, but I haven't yet seen what.

"He said the best way to learn was to be fearless," she says. "To not care about mistakes."

Of course I can't remember how I learned to guard against mistakes. Did I ever *not* care when I left a piece *en prise* or didn't know that the pawn I promoted to queen would have been more effective if I'd underpromoted it to a knight? And, of course, there was my father, who cared very much and right away about my mistakes.

"It's working," Phebe says. "Isabelle and I used to sit at the board, paralyzed with terror, and now, the more we let Clarence and those creatures at the clubs play us, the better we get."

She has moved to lean against the small dresser opposite the bed. She never sits down anywhere unless forced to eat.

"So this morning I walked into the studio, surrounded by strange girls, and I thought, I am here. I don't care what I think about. I am here."

"And it was better?"

"Yes. Much. Everything held. Everything turned."

"How about when you stayed?"

I know that she needs to do an extra adagio or some such so she won't fall behind her class at the Academy.

"I didn't," she says. "I went with Clarence to that clinic."

Right. Mr. Aldrich works with an old friend of Isabelle's. The man used to work as a doctor in a refugee camp in Thailand. There was an article about his clinic in one of the papers Mr. Aldrich makes Phebe read. Phebe was really excited about meeting him, but Isabelle declined, saying that she could do without a visit to her past.

I would like to ask Phebe about this man—what he looks like, how old he is—but I don't want my interest to be misinterpreted. If I am a little in love with Isabelle, if I am overly curious about the men she once knew, it is a secret. One I manage to keep hidden. Even, most of the time, from myself.

"Well, I have to study," I say.

"Go ahead," Phebe says. "I won't talk. I'll just stay here until I get sleepy."

I set up my board and walk the game through its last ten positions. Ugly, ugly, ugly, uglier. I make notes of different possibilities and calculate where they would have taken me. Lose, lose, lose. Unless there's something I'm refusing to see.

"I wonder if Stas will ever show up," I say, but I am talking aloud to no one. Phebe has gone.

venice, then

eleven

I GET MY PERIOD ON THE TRAIN TO VENICE. THIS HAPPENS ON occasion, even to girls who haven't been slacking off on their class schedules or eating out way too often. Mama, who thinks I should have a more regular cycle, will be thrilled. Here it is July, and I have already bled four times this year. I did not travel prepared and have to borrow from Isabelle. Of course she uses the kind sold most widely throughout Europe—tightly wrapped in cellophane and without an applicator. Ugh.

Mama is meeting us in Venice. When I told her I didn't want to miss this tournament, she said she'd be happy to meet me in Venice instead of Rome.

"It's not what I had in mind," she said. "But the important thing is to see you in your own life."

I don't know how much of my life she will find in Venice, but at least I will be in Venice to meet Vlajnik. The tournament we are going to takes place at a hotel on the Lido. Every August grandmasters of a certain ranking are invited to play one another to what Nikolai calls a bloody death.

"No one can draw a game before forty moves," he told us. "Anyone who resigns rather than fight on is never asked back."

Not my picture of a bloody death, but whatever. Vlajnik is always invited, no matter his ranking, which fluctuates wildly from year to year. Unlike most grandmasters (including the world champion), he never feels obliged to play all the tournaments that determine the ranking numbers.

"Do you want any aspirin?" Isabelle asks. "I might even have some Tylenol."

Oh, right. Cramps. I don't get those. More like a strange, unpleasant swelling.

"No, I'm okay. Thanks."

"I'm so worried he won't be there," Isabelle says.

"I thought you talked to the tournament director," I say. "That he told you Vlajnik was expected."

Not to mention some woman Clarence found in Hamburg who told him that Vlajnik had refused to audit her books, a job he did every year, because he was deep in preparation for Venice.

"There was a man in Zurich," Isabelle says. "One of the judges. He told me he'd had drinks with Vlajnik in Spain at Christmas."

"What else?" I ask, knowing Vlajnik has an old friend with a villa near Madrid. A friend with whom he has not yet become enraged. Drinks in Spain at Christmas sounds plausible, even for a man whose schedule is nothing but a rumor.

"He told me that Vlajnik said he'd already done all he could for Nikolai. That detaching him from his father was the only service he could provide."

Isabelle has known this since Zurich? That was before Nikolai and I even met. What had she been thinking as we went from city to city looking for a man who thinks he can't do anything more than he's done? Great. I look at the ceiling, which, since I am on the top berth, is only a foot away from me. Great.

"I've been hoping the man was wrong," Isabelle says.

"Maybe he was wrong," I say. "What's a judge in Zurich know?"

"He's a big-time grandmaster who'll be competing in Venice," Isabelle says.

"So he knows a lot," I say.

"At the time, I didn't know enough to care about Vlajnik," Isabelle says. "I took Clarence's word that this man would be even worse than the father."

My mother thinks we should look for Nikolai's father. Because of my Sunday night phone calls home and my letters (which she says are *most detailed*), Mama knows all about what we call The Hunt.

"The father is the one person more interested than anyone else in finding Vlajnik," she said. "Find him and you may find Vlajnik."

"He doesn't want to find Vlajnik," I said. "Nikolai's father hates Vlajnik."

"Precisely," Mama said. "You think he doesn't want Vlajnik to at least honor his promise to Nikolai?"

Huh. No, I hadn't thought that. And anyway, Nikolai's father didn't want Vlajnik anywhere near his son. Really, the idea of the father was so silly and scary and fleeting that I didn't think of it until now, trapped in a small train car with Isabelle, listening to wheels hurl us toward Italy.

"Does he ever talk to you about his father?" I ask.

"Nikolai?"

As if she and I were in the habit of discussing other boys who are notably silent on the topic of their fathers. Of course, Nikolai. Given how we have spent the last month, who else does she think I would have in mind? There is that boy Nikolai introduced us to in Amsterdam. The one he lost to (brilliantly and on Vlajnik's orders) in Salzburg. Jasper Greene.

If I were the sort of girl inclined to like a boy (or a man, as Jasper is ten or so years older than I), I would like Jasper. There was nothing spectacular about him, but the combination of his features, his unwillingness to *see* anyone he looks at, his long fingers, and his black hair all add up to . . . something. Who knows what. I think about him in a way that makes my body hurt. It's unpleasant except when it's very, very nice.

"I think Nikolai does miss his father," Isabelle says.

"Did he tell you that?" I ask, casting Jasper out of my thoughts and peering down at her.

"No," she says. "Other than normal conversation, Nikolai doesn't say much to me."

"That's because he's in love with you."

Isabelle laughs. "So you say."

"He talks to me," I say. "Around you he's, like, paralyzed with devotion."

"He admires you, Phebe," she says. "That's why he talks to you."

Oh, right. That's why. How about he's dying of loneliness and will probably perish if we don't get him suitable company?

"I think we should look for the father," I say. "Unless you know that Nikolai never wants to see him again."

"We have one card to hold over Vlajnik," Isabelle says. "That the father is gone."

"But if we can't find or force Vlajnik into holding up his end of the deal," I say, "then we should look. Like if the grandmaster in Zurich was telling you the truth."

"His father used to hit him," Isabelle says. "I've heard that from several people in a position to know."

Who would be in a position to know this? How would Nikolai have handled that kind of behavior? If his father had been hitting him, Nikolai would have left years earlier. He would have found the ugliness involved offensive. I'm sure I'm right.

"I don't believe that," I say. "His father wasn't stupid, just controlling. Would hitting someone make them play better chess?"

"I don't know," Isabelle says. "But I'd have to know before I agreed to look for him."

"I think it'd be more important to know if he misses his father," I say, pretty sure that no one on this planet will be able to make Nikolai say anything on the topic of his father and hitting.

"I'm sure he does miss him," Isabelle says. "I suspect that Nikolai's life was more, shall we say, organized when Sergey Kotalev ran it."

Sergey Kotalev. Stanislav Vlajnik. Nikolai Sergeyevich Kotalev. André Stepanovich Rogovsky.

Maybe one day I will go to the Soviet Union and . . . dance? The Company did tour there, but that was before two top Soviet dancers defected in order to work with André. The great André Rogovsky who had left Russia back when it was fighting to become the Soviet Union.

Well, one day I will go to the Soviet Union or Russia or the Kremlin or whatever it calls itself and I will . . . live. Spend time in the country that has produced all these people who have accepted that they will have to fight for what matters to them. Dance or chess. Their future. Their work. People who find a way to live for their own ideas.

I wonder if Isabelle is asleep. I listen to the steady whirring *thunk* of the train moving through the night. My grandfather was posted to Moscow once. I wonder if it was before or after Russia became the Soviet Union. Why don't I know this? I'm sure it's a fairly significant date that even a regular girl with no real ambitions would be able to cough up on demand. My uncles' daughters, for example.

Whirr-thunk. Whirr-thunk. I should sleep. *Whirr-thunk.*

Countries are artificial constructs, Mama has said to me. She has even written it in an article. I suddenly remember how in that article she used maps of Eastern Europe. Maps drawn in different decades so as to illustrate her point. Oh, my God. I see. How mortifying.

Those books my grandfather left me were all about his career. And his interests. His thoughts. Nikolai wanted to organize the books by country because he wanted me to see how the books were what was left of my grandfather's life. The books I thought were about the World Wars are books about how war changes countries and who leads them. My grandfather didn't just leave me his books. He left me evidence that he had been here.

The fire that burned down the library in Egypt is famous not because it was a huge fire, but because it destroyed evidence. Evidence of people's lives, their cultures, and their countries. Which change. Those boxes of books that Nikolai has catalogued for me provide Clarence with comfort because they are what is left of my grandfather. Aside from his ashes.

I had no idea. None.

I am not a stupid girl, but, given the evidence, who could believe otherwise? Escaping the label *stupid* has never mattered to me before. I have, until recently, built my life on the more useful intelligence within my body. Yet for months now, I have put very little value on what my body can do. If I wish to join the ranks of people who fight for what matters to them, I had better know what matters to me.

What can I put in that place where caring about a battement tendu used to reside? I count fifty-seven whirring *thunk*s before I remember: I am only fifteen. I could use the years between now and, say, twenty to discover what matters to me. If I stopped dancing I wouldn't have to turn into a regular girl.

I could turn into someone who fights for what matters to me. I could allow the nature of what matters to evolve just the way my center of balance did: through discipline and dedication. What matters could come via my thoughts. Via my grandfather's books. Via staying friends with people who are devoted to their lives.

I could save myself from having to choose between only failure and Brava. Such an idea is comforting but also terrifying. It's only an idea, I remind myself. Not a decision. I can avoid a decision for a while longer as I continue to come and go.

♛

People are playing blitz in the lobby. People my age and younger. I love blitz, but Stas has written at great length that people who are training seriously for tournaments should avoid it at all costs. Salzburg is in a month.

I turn away.

At the far end of the lobby are French doors opening out

onto a sweeping veranda beyond which is the beach. The Kings are already here. Both of them. I know because the journalists who follow them are sitting in the bar lounge on the left side of the hotel entrance.

The blitz is set up at tables on the right, where there is no bar, only plenty of places to look out at the garden, which seemed endless as we walked through it to the hotel entrance. Phebe, who has been watching the players, suddenly turns. I feel her fly past me.

Mr. Aldrich and Isabelle have gone ahead to the reception desk, located halfway between the views of the ocean and of the garden. This is probably, for most people, a very nice place to stay, but I wouldn't want to play a tournament here. Two weeks of walking in and out of this place, trying not to see it? Thank you, no.

And it's while I'm having this particular thought that I see him. Stepping out of the noonday light from the glass doors. He is without his jacket, but his tie is held neatly by its usual clip. His hands slip out of his pockets as he strides toward me. *A gentleman does not interrupt the line of his clothes.* I can hear him say this as clearly as on the day he did say it. Not to me, but to a rumpled grandmaster from Romania.

The other players call Stas "the champion dandy" but only behind his back. Even if he is having an off-year he stores up every slight, punishing the offenders when he returns to his talents by blowing them—elegantly—off the board. He dresses as if time has never changed since he was young, and some like to say this is what makes him so memorable. But, in truth, Stas throws a shadow on us all, because while time has changed, he can still play as if every new twist in the game were his invention.

He sees me, I have no doubt. I have the flashing lights and the thoughts of caution, but I begin to walk toward him. I should have worn my suit, I think. I should have let Isabelle take me shopping.

"Kolya!"

And though he has not broken his stride nor caught my eye, I am sure it is him calling my name. But it is Phebe, pulling at my elbow.

"Kolya, guess who's here already," she says, all of her pointing away from where my life is.

He brushes past me. I am less than air.

"Stas," I say. Not to him, but to her, turning myself toward the direction in which her energy is flying. "That was Stas."

"Vlajnik? That man going out the front?"

"Yes."

"Clarence!" she calls. "He's here!"

And she is out the door before either Mr. Aldrich or Isabelle have time to turn their heads from the receptionist. I walk through the blitz tables to the windows and push the gauzy curtains aside. Phebe is giving Stas the full treatment. All of her pouncing and pointing and pulling and talking. His English is better than mine, but surely he is pretending not to understand a word.

A hand touches my shoulder.

"Nikolai?" a woman's voice says. "I'm Maggie Knight, Phebe's mother. My God, look at her making such a fuss."

What Phebe has going for her, if she can guess it, is that Stas has a horror of scenes. His number-one reason, I now think, for his requiring that my father vanish.

"I'm sorry," I say, turning to the woman who I'd forgotten existed. "I'm very pleased to meet you, Mrs. Knight."

And I am. With the part of me that hasn't fallen off of the earth, I am very pleased to meet the person behind the *Mama* who crops up repeatedly in Phebe's orders and ideas.

"That would be my mother. You will have to learn how to use *Ms.*," she says. "Here he comes."

She does not mean Stas, who is still outside, now talking with both Phebe *and* Isabelle, but rather Mr. Aldrich.

"Hello, Clarence."

"Maggie."

"Tell me, what magic have you wrought to get her so worked up over something aside from her feet?"

"She came to me this way," Mr. Aldrich says.

"No," *Ms.* Knight says. "Her letters and calls home are full of that will to change someone else's world. That comes only from you."

Mr. Aldrich reaches past her to pull aside the curtain, which I had let fall back into place. Without speaking, he and I turn our eyes back outside, to where my life is. Isabelle is shaking Stas's hand and keeping a grip on Phebe, who radiates thwarted urgency. No one has told her that delay will often produce better results. It is good for Stas to have a measure of both Phebe and Isabelle. I could not have chosen better representatives to prove how far I have traveled since last we met.

TWELVE

V<small>LAJNIK HAS AGREED TO MEET WITH US ON HIS FIRST OFF-DAY</small>. H<small>E</small> has to play both Kings between now and then. And Jasper Greene, who, Nikolai informs me, has a good chance of winning while everyone else competes to their own bloody deaths. I make no mention to anyone of how Jasper makes my breath catch and my heart pound. It is the most enjoyable secret I have ever had.

Jasper ignores everyone but Nikolai. Nikolai follows Jasper everywhere. How nice they have each other.

I have dinner with my mother each night, and we are sharing a room, but that's about it. It's mostly my fault. I am not ready to answer her questions about how I am. As much as possible, I avoid being alone with her. Mama is used to me and has learned when to force an issue and when to leave well enough alone.

My mother keeps busy watching the games and talking to the other journalists, one of whom is a good friend from when we lived in London. She asks him to get her a pass so she can watch the games from the pressroom every morning and afternoon. I ask her if she is that interested or simply prowling for information about Nikolai's father, but she says it's all just fascinating. A high-level chess tournament is like a little laboratory of human behavior.

Funny how she's never found any human behavior worth studying at the Academy. Funny how I haven't either. I am hard pressed to think of anyone—at the Academy or the Company—who interests me above and beyond how they move. A wandering thought with which I need to spend some time.

There's not a lot to do on the Lido if you don't play chess, gamble (Venice's casinos are here), or sit in the sun (the beach is here too.) Every morning, Mama or Clarence or Isabelle buys me a day pass so I can zip around on the vaporetti. Most days, however, I get off of line 6, which is the direct steamer from Lido Island to Venice and which stops near San Marco's Square. From there I just walk until I am so lost I am forced to find my way back to the canal.

I am not taking class while I am here. It was Mademoiselle's idea. When we returned to Geneva, I immediately went to the studio. I was better in class than I had thought possible. I even stayed after. Not bad. Not good, but not bad.

I couldn't convince myself that it mattered either way. Or that it didn't. At some point during the days we were home, I realized I was happier to be back in a familiar city than in a familiar dance class. Still, I made sure to tell Mademoiselle I would be in Venice for two weeks and to ask if she knew of a place where I could take class.

"I do have a friend who lives in Venice now," Mademoiselle said. "Only I don't think she teaches."

"She might know someone who does," I said, thinking how there was no way I was leaving Geneva without a destination for my body.

"Have you ever been to Venice, Phebe?" she asked. "To Italy?"

"Sort of," I said, which was the short answer.

Long answer: My mother had a job in Rome when I was little, but we didn't travel much in Italy. She'd transferred to Rome from Berlin (where I was born), stayed two years, and then got a transfer to London. Two years later we were in New York. Two years after that, my grandfather died and Mama left the wire service for the magazine.

"There are such things as vacations, you know," Mademoiselle told me. "I can't think of anything more instructive than going to Venice and enjoying yourself."

"We're going to a chess tournament," I said, although I knew she already knew.

"You're going to be in Venice for two weeks," she said. "Don't even pack your shoes. Have a good time. I'll be here when you get back."

Well, of course, I packed my shoes. But they are still in my suitcase while I work as hard as possible on having a good time. For 100 lire I can buy cut-up pieces of coconut near the Rialto. For 350 lire I can sit in almost any café and take as long as I like drinking pear juice.

When I can find one, I buy the *Herald Tribune* (it sells out really fast in tourist-attraction places like Venice). I read it in a café or on steps overlooking any number of canals or squares. The leader of the military coup has been shot and his generals are debating who should now take charge. I can find no news about the flood that caused so much economic devastation. But there was an earthquake in India. It takes days to dig out all the people.

Story after story, with no mention whatsoever of an

important and prestigious chess tournament. When I read the paper I feel very alone. Except for when I feel totally immersed in what is taking place thousands of miles away. I am still a part of Nikolai's small world while staying in contact with the larger one into which I will, at some point, need to enter.

I get a lot of attention from men here. It's a bit shocking, but after a while I don't even notice the *bella, bella* that men say to me as I pass. It doesn't appear to have anything to do with me so much as with my being a girl. A girl by herself. I walk without making eye contact. I read. I sit.

It's so hot on some days that the only places where one can cool down are churches. Most of them seem more like cathedrals, and all of them are named after saints or apostles. The best are the ones with marble everywhere and high ceilings that soak up cool air and send it down in erratic blasts. Until today, my favorite was San Maurizo, not far from the Fenice Theater. I come upon San Trovaso by accident, walking circles through the city and soaking from the heat. Once inside, I sit without moving for two hours.

I don't believe in God or anything like that, but someone is in this building. Someone besides me and the people visible to my eye. Mama says God is only for people who can't accept random acts of fate. I've always puzzled over this. Not enough to ask her, but enough to wonder and ask myself during these two hours: What's a random act of fate? Versus just a plain act of fate? And what do people who can accept their fate, random or otherwise, believe in?

André has an icon in his office, and a lot of the principal

dancers at the Company cross themselves while standing in the wings, waiting to go on. Nikolai wears a small pendant around his neck with the words *save and protect* written across it. In Russian. I asked him to translate, but I never said anything after, as the words struck me as distinctly religious and therefore deeply private.

When I finally leave San Trovaso, I walk all the way up to the train station and then follow all the signs back down to San Marco's. As I come into the square, I ignore all the people and tables and pigeons and vendors and I stare just as hard as I can at the basilica.

If there is a God, I don't think He or She wishes to communicate directly. Fine. Why should God be a performer? It would make us all audience members. I make my way to one of the square's many cafés, selecting a chair with its back to the basilica.

I order my pear juice and watch. The dirty white buildings that invite one to explore beyond them. The people who are alone and writing postcards. The people who are alone and just sitting, facing what I have my back to. The people with companions.

It occurs to me, after a while, that I am behaving like someone who is waiting. This will not do. I will have to make my own decisions. I can't sit around hoping for external guidance.

I leave 350 lire on the wobbly tin table and walk over to where I can board line 6 back to the Lido. I think how I should take care of my own transportation in the mornings. A day pass is extravagant in a way that I don't find appealing.

* * *

According to the board in the lobby, Jasper is, as of his third round, four points behind one of the Kings and five behind Stas and the other King. Soon, I know, I will have to learn their names. Nikolai's favorite is the one who does not bribe the trainers of the other one. That King has a very nice mother. I know because she has spent the little free time she has talking to Mama and Isabelle. Nikolai ignores all the buzz and fuss directed at him since our arrival, but I believe he likes it.

Who would have thought? It's not just a man like Vlajnik who is flattered by attention. Everyone likes to hear Brava, not just dancers and other eccentrics. I watch the kids playing blitz in the lobby, willing them to be flattered by my attention. They are too busy slamming their clocks and almost throwing their pieces into position to notice that they have an audience. Alas.

"Jasper has an off-day tomorrow."

I look to my left. It's Nikolai, sitting quietly in the chair next to mine.

"How come his is earlier than Vlajnik's?"

"You get to pick," Nikolai says. "Stas doesn't like to break until he feels almost broken. Jasper likes to spread himself out more evenly."

"Oh," I say. I want to ask how it is that Jasper can spend all day playing chess and then stay up more than half the night working with Nikolai, tearing apart finished games as a way of preparing for games that don't exist yet. But I know. Jasper can do it the same way I once dreamed of getting up, going to class, going to rehearsal, more rehearsal, having a break, warming up (again), going to wardrobe, standing by for curtain cues, and performing. Every day for the rest of my life. Until I too, like Stas, felt broken. "I'm sorry, what?"

"Jasper wants to see you dance."

"Because?" I find this unlikely, as I am not convinced Jasper knows who I am. I don't add up to anything for him the way he does for me.

"He's never been to the ballet."

"Oh, come on," I say. "His parents are rich people in Boston. They took him to the ballet. Believe me."

"They might have tried to," Nikolai says. "You don't really understand how isolated we keep ourselves. Jasper has never seen any ballet. Now he's willing. If you will do it."

"We're in Venice," I say. "There are at least four theaters here. It's the height of tourist season. I'm sure I can find tickets to something that will give him a fair idea of what's involved."

"Jasper has one hour to spare tomorrow," Nikolai says. "In the afternoon. I told him we had to be a little flexible, as you need to ask for the studio space."

"Where?"

"Wherever you're taking class."

"I'm not taking class," I say. "I'm supposed to be enjoying myself."

Even as I say this, I am going over how easy it would be. Ask the hotel to hunt down a vacant studio, ask Clarence for the rental fee. I have a tape of the music right inside my highly prized, brand-new Walkman. I would do the third girl solo from *Quartets*. The girl in the white leotard. I know this part inside and out. I need three hours to practice, and then they could come whenever they chose.

121

"Okay," I say, standing up. "I'd better get busy."

"Really?" he says, looking up at me.

Is he surprised or pleased? "Would you take your glasses off?" I ask him.

"Yes," he says, taking them off as he stands. We are the exact same height. "Why?"

"I want to see something," I say. His eyes are pale blue. They fit well with the rest of his face, which is pale, commands attention, and remains determinedly closed to scrutiny.

"I know it's a lot to ask," Nikolai says. "An impromptu performance and all. But Jasper is interested."

"In return, I get to watch him play Vlajnik," I say. "And you have to sit with me and explain what they're doing and why."

"Yes," he says. "I'll try."

"Me too," I say, motioning for him to put his glasses back on.

What in the world was I thinking? As if I could possibly discover anything. As if simply looking would allow one to slip past Nikolai's guard. I leave him standing near the blitz, blinking his eyes back into focus as I go off in search of a studio.

I never see Phebe here. I would have to search for her. Each day she goes out into the city to explore, and I stay in the hotel. Jasper has, as he promised, put me to work. The few times we have walked past her, it is as if he does not see her. For her part, Phebe likes Jasper enough to act as if they have never met. I noticed just how unwillingly her eyes grew wide and her mouth smiled when they shook hands in Amsterdam.

She should have someone she can like only from afar. I

would imagine that Jasper would be impossible for a girl to like up close. Also, at twenty-seven, he is too old for her. Which is precisely why she likes him.

It's strange to realize that I have known Jasper for eight years. Exactly half of my life. It feels both longer and shorter than that.

"Time whips by without remorse," Stas told me once.

Yes, I suppose it does.

For Jasper, time is running out. He says he has five to eight years left to compete at the highest level. He was a candidate for the world championship two years ago, but the Kings snuffed him out. He's a very strong player, except when he's not. The problem with Jasper, as he'd be the first to say, is that he has little control of when he's strong and when he's not. Too often, he allows things to follow him onto the board.

The thing with Stas, for example. Jasper won when we played in Salzburg, but he felt humiliated about how he won. There's no glory in winning when your opponent is playing to lose. He blamed Stas more than he blamed me. Thereafter, each time Jasper faced Stas in a game, he felt that he wasn't playing a game. He was settling a score. His dignity depended on his ability to win. And so he did.

"You gave me a huge advantage," Jasper says. "Stas is a much stronger player than I am."

Of course, Stas will stay stronger if Jasper never overcomes his conviction that he's not as strong. Stas has already lost to Jasper three times this year. But Jasper maintains it is not due to his own strength.

"It's because I remember the game in Salzburg," Jasper tells me. "All those emotions come together and focus my mind on exacting a payment."

His big terror now is that the disbelief and the fury and the humiliation he felt are fading.

"We must find something you can rely on," I say. It is past three in the morning, and we have gone over all the different ways we can think of to play black against his opponent tomorrow afternoon. "Something off the board that is tangible and consistently makes your game sharp and clear."

"Like your father did for you?" Jasper asks. "I think not. I'd rather know I'm not the stronger player than have that kind of lunatic at my side."

If I refused to keep company with everyone who saw my father as a lunatic, I'd be a lot lonelier than necessary. I try to explain.

"At first my father did it for me," I say, "which gave me good habits for study and competition."

"That's certainly true." Jasper has already wanted to break twice, both times far before I think we have worked enough.

"Then I had Stas," I say. "All that mattered was how the board looked. I replaced my father with beautiful patterns."

"Which are on the board," Jasper says. "I need something off the board. Concrete, that I can call upon. You said so yourself."

"Patterns can be found everywhere," I tell him. "If you play intending to make your game fit into a bigger pattern, you can rely on that. It will guide you."

Except, of course, when you can't. Like my win in Hamburg. A private lapse that I need to analyze with Stas, not casually discuss with Jasper.

"Beautiful patterns are not the same as winning ones," he says. "They're just not."

He goes over to the board and rearranges the pieces to where they stood in a game the two Kings recently played. He walks the pieces through to the draw at which the Kings finally arrived. Brutal, bloody, hideous. Sacrifices for positional advantage that resulted in material loss.

"The problem with you, Kolya," Jasper says, "is that your father put too much pressure on you to win."

"It was just the right amount," I say.

My father used to say that the right amount of pressure was the amount I felt I could not bear. *More pressure than you can bear is what life holds,* he'd say. *Get used to it.*

"It was so much too much," Jasper says, "that you took the first chance at escape you had. Playing beautifully is not the same as winning."

"You've missed the point," I say.

"Here is the point," Jasper says. "When Stas loses, he is a loser. Not a beautiful player."

"No," I say. "That's not it at all."

"Yes," he says. "All your talk of winning being beside the point is just a way to avoid confronting that the best chess is the game that wins."

"No," I say, but one can refuse to see what's there for just so long. My ugly win shows up on the board I picture mentally. I finally see it for what it is: a breakthrough game. They've happened to me before. I'd spend hours, days, weeks, and months studying. All the information I crammed into my head would remain there as just that: information. Until the game, when I could suddenly see ahead faster. Grasp more possibilities and calculate their results.

"Yes," Jasper says. "What is there off the board that's more beautiful than a win you've created?"

What does this say about Stas, then? No. Oh, no. I wanted to replace my father with a chess teacher, and I made a bad choice. Very bad. Except I have an answer for Jasper.

"I have a friend," I say. "She's a dancer."

"A girl," he says. "Well, Kolya, you're sixteen years old. You should have a crush on a girl. It will pass."

I know better than to volunteer any details about what I have locked up where. A crush, as Americans call it, is what I have on Isabelle. Phebe is my friend.

"Ballet can be more beautiful than chess," I say.

I almost mean it. All of the pressure my father exerted is still here. There are times when I'd do anything to escape it. Even giving up chess so as to admire something—anything—else. It's not that I am unaware of the pressures on Phebe. It's that the results she has are at once more nebulous (who wins or loses in ballet?) and less definitive. After all, what's really at stake in a performance? Jasper laughs and then stops, suddenly frowning.

"No one can play the way you can and prefer anything else," he says. "It's impossible."

"Don't you ever get tired?" I ask him. "Tired of being afraid?"

"I'm afraid all the time," he says. "I'm afraid I'll spend the rest of my life training other people for their best games."

This is the most agreed-upon assessment of Jasper's talents. Strong player, not strong enough.

"But tomorrow you win," I say, gesturing to the board we have banged up and the books we have combed through.

I straighten up what I can. We've done a lot, but we don't have anything off the board for him to rely on. I tell him that when he takes his off-day, I'll show him the best game I ever played and take him to see Phebe dance.

"Who is Phebe?" he asks.

"My friend," I say. "You've met her."

"Oh, the daughter," Jasper says without interest. "I thought your best game was against me."

"I lost that one," I tell him. "I have in mind the best game I ever won."

When I get back to my room, I lie down on the floor with a cold, wet washcloth over my eyes. Just in case. If I make it to twenty-seven, I want to be playing my own best games. If this means never winning, well, perhaps I will get used to losing. If I'm afraid all the time I want there to be a reason. A reason off the board. A reason behind both the fear and the playing well.

One might assume I want my father back, but I know I am holding out for something—someone—worth more. Just what or who, I don't yet know.

THIRTeen

OF COURSE, NOTHING IS EVER AS EASY TO EXECUTE AS IT IS TO THINK up. Clarence gives me the rental fee without comment but mentions it in passing to Mama. Who brings it up at dinner. Which we are having out and alone. Nikolai eats with Jasper at a table in the players' section of the hotel dining room. My father and Isabelle alternate eating with them, going out alone, or joining Mama and me.

Tonight I am back to counting bites, as tomorrow I face my leotard. And a mirror. Mama has taken me to a place where I can choose between pounded, breaded veal or a bowl of pasta with ham and cream. I opt for the veal.

"It's hardly following Elena's instructions if you rent a space to give yourself class," Mama says. "That's not really taking a break."

"It's just one day," I say.

"When you join the Company, you'll never have a day off," Mama says. "Even on nights when the theater is dark, you'll take class or be in rehearsal."

"You're right," I say. "If I joined the Company, I'd never have a day off. Not even an off-day."

"Take them now, Phebe," she says. "It's not just your crazy mother talking. Elena is a stand-in for André. Listen to them."

This is not a factory. I can't think of anything more instructive. You are not a product. I'll be here when you get back.

"I have listened," I say, hoping I can forgive her for how happy she will be at my news.

"Then spend the full two weeks without doing a plié," Mama says. "Give yourself space to think."

"I have been thinking," I say, pushing my plate away. "In the fall, I might want to go to the International School. The one in Geneva. You don't have to know French. It can be, like, one of the things you study."

When we were in Geneva, I did more than drag myself to class. I made a list of what mattered to me there—my father, Isabelle, my grandfather's books, which are his history and therefore mine. There is also a school designed to teach me everything I have been unremarkable at learning. It all adds up to a lot.

"Oh, my," Mama says. "I had no idea."

"Isabelle's office has an internship," I say. "It's a glorified messenger girl, but within a month I'll probably know more things than I do now."

"You can come home and build a new life for yourself," Mama says. "There's plenty to do at home."

"I want to stay," I say. "It seems important."

"How much does this have to do with the boy?"

"I'm not sure," I tell her, a rush of gratitude flooding through me. How good of her to guess. To know more about me than I do, even as I am turning into a stranger. "It's mostly that he was the first clue I had that I could live in some other way."

"His life is hideously crippled by his ambition," Mama says.

"I know," I say, wondering if she will always refuse to see the benefits that allegiance to one thing brings. If someone wants only what they have to offer, chess and ballet are worth all that must be given up. "But it's his life. It's his choice."

129

"I gather that liking him has led you to fixate less on your dance career," she says.

"I don't like him in the way you mean," I say, "but he is important to me."

"I suspect you'd like him if he gave you half a chance," Mama says.

No, the person I'd like if he gave me half a chance is Jasper. Jasper is good-looking and elusive in a way I understand that boys are supposed to be. The person who matters to me is Nikolai. Because of Nikolai's life, I can see all the ways I want something new and different for myself.

"If he had the time for that kind of thing, he wouldn't be important," I say. "I have no desire to be friends with someone who wants a girlfriend."

"We have no idea what Vlajnik will do or say," Mama says. "You could find yourself in Switzerland with only Clarence for company."

"It's my plan to have a lot of options," I say, enjoying the echo of her words. She has always told me how dancing limited my options. "It's an accident that Nikolai's life is the one I noticed."

"Like it was an accident," Mama says, "that the first time you saw the ballet, you fell in love with it."

"Random acts of fate," I say.

"Not quite," she says. "More like you are your father's daughter. Not just mine."

"No," I say. "I love you much more."

"Phebe, I'm not questioning that," she says. "You love us as you will."

She has always said I must choose my life. Now that I am actually doing that, I want her to see it.

"My decision about dancing is only that," I say, hoping to explain. "It's not about Clarence. Or even Nikolai. I want to stay because of me."

"I have to give this some thought," she says. "And talk to your father. It's not entirely your decision."

"I know," I say. "But you have always made excellent decisions about difficult things."

It takes her a while to realize that I am quoting her own father, but I can see her face light up when she sees what I mean.

"I miss him every day," she says. "His belief in me was like a shield."

A shield. That would be a worthy goal for what is left of my dedication, discipline, and zeal. I could turn my very will to dance—to think—into a shield. Not just for Nikolai, God knows, but for my own life.

Quartets is the first ballet André conceived when he came to America. He was trying to start a school and a company. The dancers he taught had been initially trained by others. He had to do everything over again from scratch. So he picked his favorite piece of music and choreographed variations to mirror it. He didn't want a story, but an emphasis on what happened in class as he retaught his dancers to hold themselves this way or that.

I have forced myself through an hour-long barre and spent three more hours reviewing what I know and refining as I am able the places where I would have, some day, learned to shine. With my Italian limited to *per favore* and *grazie* but my smile endless, I have procured two comfortable chairs from the doctor's office down the hallway. When my audience arrives, I can tell that Jasper doesn't recognize me. Of course, the one time we met I was dressed in street clothes.

I have cued the music up for about a minute before my entrance. They will have to settle for watching me stand, motionless, on the left side of the room. I move and breathe. I dance. It's not the best dancing I have ever done, but for what I mean it to be—a measured moment in time, which does indeed conspire against us—it is the best dancing I will do.

They don't clap, which is just as well, as I would be embarrassed. I cross the studio to turn the tape player off. There is sweat pouring off of every surface my body has. Jasper stands up.

"We should have brought you flowers," he says. "I had no idea it would be so beautiful."

This is a nice thing for him to say, and I like how he is looking at me. As if I am a creature as far removed from a regular girl as is humanly possible. And, more importantly, as if he is seeing me for the very first time.

"I told you it was beautiful," Nikolai says to Jasper, who is still, well, kind of staring at me. Or was. He turns toward Nikolai.

"It's intricate and astonishing," Jasper says. "But not beautiful like chess."

"No," I say, knowing better than to tell him that it is. Beautiful like chess.

"I told him that ballet could be more beautiful," Nikolai says.

Of course it *could* be. I gesture to the studio.

"With lights, an orchestra, and the whole dance, perhaps," I say. "But just me up against chess? With you two as judges?"

"Are you so enamored with people?" Jasper asks.

"You mean, do I like people?" I ask him, wondering what he is asking me. Is it obvious that I have a pathetic schoolgirl crush on him?

"Yes, do you have affection for strangers?"

"Um, no," I say. I think of my cousins who live cheerfully as regular girls. Of the small-boned girls in Geneva with perfect English. "I don't have affection for strangers. I don't even like more than, say, seven people in the whole entire world."

"Seven is a lot for people like us," Jasper says. "Maybe it's not so many for you and your dance."

"I don't know what dance has to do with people," I say, starting to think I don't like Jasper after all. I'm just attracted to him. A feeling I don't want to have for men whom I neither like nor know.

"Jasper thinks you must have more affection for people than you admit," Nikolai says in the quiet, reserved voice he uses around Isabelle. "Because you want to spend your life bringing them so much pleasure."

I get a towel out from underneath my folded-up clothes and wipe my face. Ballet does bring people pleasure. I have, over the years, forgotten that this is the whole point of the exercise. The pleasure involved for both performer and audience.

"Do you play chess for pleasure?" I ask, a question for Nikolai, but it is Jasper who replies.

"I play to live," he says. "It is like a drug. And it is the same for Kolya. He fears to believe it. Just as he fears to win."

"You don't seem afraid to win," I say.

"I have been distracted by what is beautiful," Nikolai says.

"Thank you for the performance," Jasper says. "One day I will see you in a real theater."

Probably not, I think. "Good luck tomorrow," I say.

He plays Vlajnik tomorrow. Then Vlajnik faces his second King. Then his much anticipated off-day.

"Please take that back," Jasper says. "Now. Right away."

I look at Nikolai. Take what back?

"Jasper has no faith in luck," he says. "He thinks we should be prepared to play beyond luck's domain. It's bad luck to wish him luck."

"Oh, I'm so sorry," I say. "I take it back. I beg your pardon."

"It's fine," Jasper says. "I assumed you knew. It has no power if it's a good-luck wish made by accident."

These are very strange people. And still I am . . . enamored with them. After they leave, I cue the music up and dance again, this time facing the mirror instead of the two chairs by the door. My steps are fast. They are clear. I am inside of something beautiful. I am part of it. When I am done, I make my révérence to the empty room. So this is the world I am choosing to leave. So, good-bye.

Phebe and I watch from the pressroom. I dislike this point of view, but how else will I possibly explain the game to her?

There's no talking inside of the playing hall and too much talking in here. Monitors hang from the ceiling. Telex machines compete with phones for table space. Journalists crowd around grandmasters, who study the board and give ill-informed analysis.

To be fair to them, it's very hard to penetrate a game happening between top players. The people who best understand what is happening are the two men playing. Afterward, they might explain or they might not. When I study games like this, I know that I am understanding only a shadow of what has transpired.

Phebe looks all around, waves to her mother, and then plants herself in front of the monitor farthest away from the phones and telexes. We watch the first twelve moves in silence until Stas brings out his queen and Jasper responds by moving his bishop. Which of course Stas follows with his queen.

"It's a victory for Vlajnik," a previous United States champion says. "Look at the combination he is preparing to play."

Which one? I see at least three or four he could have in mind. How can we know?

"No, black is clearly ahead in position," says the current British champion.

This man and I have been avoiding each other. While we were in London, my father accused him of robbing us. All the man did was prevent me from playing in a tournament open only to grandmasters. But we were new escapees from a so-called Evil Empire. My father was able to make the case, despite the facts, that a chess prodigy was being denied his freedom to play. The press was hard on their champion. Since that time he and I have never spoken.

After careful study, Jasper retreats with his queenside knight. The journalists look at the board and pester all the grandmasters in the room for information.

"They don't know what's happening," Phebe says.

"It's hard," I say. "I barely know."

"Let's get out of here, then," she says. "We'll watch in the hall."

"We can't talk there," I say.

"We don't need to talk," she says. "We need to be there for them."

I follow her out of the pressroom.

"The King you like best," she says, as we cross the lobby to the hall. "I've noticed his mother is never out of sight when he plays. I heard that during the last champion match, she even slept in his hotel room so he wouldn't be alone."

"But he was alone," I say. "When you play, it is only you. All alone."

"Except for the guy you're playing," she says.

"When you're really good," I say, "you play against your own weaknesses more than your opponent's strengths."

I wonder how long before I am really good. Good enough for pure chess. When did Stas's strength become his most damaging blind spot? How vigilant will I need to be during my life?

Phebe pauses at the door to the hall. "Whom do you want to win? Stas or Jasper?"

"I don't know," I say. I realize this can only mean my chess no longer depends on Stas being triumphant.

"I'll watch out for Jasper, then," she says. "You take Stas."

"How do you mean?" This happens a lot with Phebe. Her

English often makes me feel the way I did when I still needed a translator. "What is *to take Stas*?"

"We're pretending they need us," she says. "It will be the only way to get through. For me, at least."

It's a long game. Stas builds a slight advantage and never loses it. Jasper plays very well, but not well enough. I guess the emotions from Salzburg really have faded.

When they are done, during the postmortem, Jasper looks like he's going to throw up. Every time he tries to offer a possibility, Stas is there with a better one. I dislike the postmortem even more than the pressroom. It is the height of cruelty to ask men who have spent hours trying to out-play each other to suddenly explain, in a calm and civilized manner, what they had been thinking during the heat of battle.

"This is awful," Phebe says. "Poor Jasper. Can't he just excuse himself?"

"He will shortly," I say. "But he has to do it for a little bit."

"I'll wait for you in the lobby," she says. "Ugh."

After a few more minutes of polite torture, it is not Jasper who calls it off, but Stas, saying he has pressing business. As he walks past, he motions for me to follow. I am so startled and caught in the eyes of the other spectators that it takes me a moment to obey.

I arrive outside the hall and see Stas talking to Phebe in the bar lounge. She is shaking her head.

"Kolya," Stas calls. "Come. Now we talk."

I walk toward them and hear Phebe say, "Clarence and Isabelle need to be here. We can't discuss Nikolai's life without them."

"But you were free to assault me in the garden without them, no?" Stas asks. He looks tired, the way one does after a hard game, but he sounds amused. "Come, let us all go outside. You have gone to great lengths to find me. Now I am here."

"Not without Clarence and Isabelle."

Either Stas will consent to teach me or he won't. Either I have something to learn from him or I don't. We hardly need Mr. Aldrich or Isabelle for this.

"They went to Murano," I say. "Isabelle wanted to see the glass."

"You shouldn't call your father by his Christian name," Stas says to Phebe. "It breeds an unnecessary distance."

"It's an appropriate distance," she says. "We met late in life."

"Let's go outside," I say, fearing that if we get derailed by Phebe's family history we will never return to my life.

We go out into the garden, following Stas to a bench in the shade. Phebe, of course, does not sit down, but remains standing before us, shifting her weight from foot to foot.

"So, tell me, young lady, what it is you were so anxious to impress upon me last week?"

"Don't you play one of the Kings tomorrow?" she asks. "I thought that's why we had to wait before you would deign to receive us."

This is not good. Stas hates sarcasm. He hates any kind of disrespect.

"Phebe, please," I say. "He is receiving us now."

"It's all right, Kolya," Stas says. "She is entitled to her questions."

"Thank you," she says, settling on her back foot and sounding more docile.

"I play the younger one tomorrow," he tells her. "I am very familiar with his strengths. Unless he makes a mistake, I will not beat him."

The King to whom Stas refers does make mistakes. None I can see on my own, but I have read articles that point out and explain them. The trick, it seems, to playing this King is to prepare so as to spot his small, subtle mistakes. Not to wait for him to make one that is easily discerned during the pressures of a game. That will never happen.

"So it doesn't matter if we break your concentration," Phebe says. "It's his concentration you want to break."

"Precisely," Stas says.

"Well, you know what we want to discuss," she says. "Your end of the bargain. Nikolai did something for you and now you have to . . ." She trails off and looks at me. "What do you want from him?"

I am a different player than I was last September. I am sure of it. If he had taught me then, I would also be a different player. Better? No. Worse? No. But different.

"I don't know," I say.

"Yes, I thought so," Stas says. "That man in Hamburg, he was my spy. It's always useful. The game against a blind man."

"The blind man?" I ask, spinning my mind back, far back, beyond my ugly win.

"You had no mercy," he says. "Your game has gone on. Without me. Also, without your father."

Did I erase that particular game? I have to do that sometimes. Review all the material I have saved and see what I still need and what can now go. After that night in Jasper's room, what did I send away? Wait. My lights flash. Here it is. I see the sleeve of his jacket. The small feather in the brim of his hat. Not his face. I must have been afraid of his blindness.

The board I carry in my mind assembles its pieces and I watch the game play itself out. This was the breakthrough game. The following one was simply the game I noticed. I look at them both now. They have their own beauty. If I look deeper, there are patterns there.

"When I saw the game," Stas says, "no one had to tell me that you had returned to staring off into space."

"What are you talking about?" Phebe demands. "Nikolai always stares off into space. So he can see the board. The one he keeps in his head."

I pull myself away from my newly discovered brilliance. I didn't know she knew I did this.

"Stas doesn't like the way playing in your head makes you look," I tell her.

"Who wants to be in a room full of men staring into space?" Stas asks her. "We are chess players. If we want to see the board, we look at it."

"Why should you care how he looks?" Phebe demands. "We want you to care how he plays."

"This is a brutal business, young lady," Stas says. "We are only as good as our last win. Tomorrow, I will be murdered by a man almost half my age."

"Murder is perhaps excessive," she says. "You might lose."

"No, Phebe," I say. "He's right. That's what it feels like."

Certainly, I feared my father after a loss. But more I feared the way my hands shook, the way my words sounded slurred, and how when I looked in the mirror I was not always there.

"So if I am preoccupied with how things look," Stas says, "you will understand that this is how I manage to get up every morning knowing I will die."

"That's what I want," I say, belatedly answering Phebe's question.

"Tell us," Stas says.

"You have to do it," Phebe says to him. "He sent his father away for you."

"We shall see," Stas says to her. To me, he says, "You simply traded him for a more attractive model."

She can be unrelenting, I realize for the first time. I have met her at too young an age. She would be a prize for someone who knew how to employ her talents, but I am ill equipped for the gift one could have in Phebe. I have known it all along. Thus the headache, always triggered when I am faced with a problem I initially see no way to solve.

"How do I manage the pressure?" I ask.

"Where does the pressure come from?" Stas asks.

"It's always there," I say. "It's there when I wake up. It's there with the board."

"Yes. Some thought it would vanish when your father did," Stas says. "It's why no exception was made for you in Salzburg. Your playing was brilliant, and some argued you should be made a grandmaster on its basis."

But I had consented to lose. This is what I saw in Jasper's

eyes all through the game. There was disbelief, horror, shame. But mostly judgment. For I was losing.

"The pressure can't vanish," Phebe says. "It comes from having to be the best he's ever been. Not just against you *patzers*, but against himself."

She's drastically overstepped. A patzer is a dull, ignorant chess player. Stas is a former world champion. Certain etiquette must be observed.

"Try to remember that you are the daughter of a diplomat," I say softly.

"Most especially against himself," Stas says. "Kolya, you have been graced. If you can manage the pressure, you'll be what chess looks like. If you can't, you will have to settle for a variation."

"That's it?" Phebe asks. "That's the sum of your help?"

"Sit down," I tell her. "You're making us tired."

Stas stands. In the fading summer light, he looks much older than I imagine forty-five to be. Some say he lost his title in exchange for certain privileges. Others believe he lost it the way we all lose. There are rumors that he went on a hunger strike for thirty-seven days to get the privileges he has. I suppose that either way one might assume he lost years off his life when he fought so hard for it.

"It's the sum of my help," he says. "I am sorry to have fallen so below your expectations."

"I didn't mean it to sound that way," she says. "I beg your pardon."

"Not at all," he says. "I hope your Nikolai is clever enough to arrange for us all to see more of you."

I'm not. There's no way. I am better prepared to find a way to run from Jasper's fate than I am able to tie Phebe's life to mine. She sits down on the bench in Stas's place. We watch him walk through the garden to the hotel.

"I'm sorry if I seemed rude," she says. "I'd just put so much value in his helping me."

"You mean me," I say. "Not you. How could he help you? The man's a genius, but he can't dance."

"I mean what I mean," she says.

I'd laugh, but I am too disappointed. It's hard to remember that I once believed that asking Isabelle (with just the right words) to help find Vlajnik would be the magic needed to release me.

fourteen

I AM, IN FACT, MUCH MORE CHEERFUL THAN I LET ON ABOUT THE
encounter with Vlajnik. Nikolai has the goods. He is the real
deal. He doesn't lack the talent or the will. He is merely confused about how to manage them. Not the best news, but not
the death knell it would be if he had told Vlajnik that he was
thinking of, say, other things.

"I'm getting better without noticing," Nikolai says.

"That's good," I say. "Isn't it?"

"I'm not sure," he says. "I need to be working harder so
that I know what I know when I know it."

"You're already a grandmaster," I say. "He told you as
much."

Nikolai shakes his head and slips his fingers up to press
his eyes shut under his glasses. He should have a new, less
clunky pair. Isabelle wants to buy him new clothes. I'll tell her
to put glasses on the list.

"I need to spend more time with it," he says. "But I understand everything that happened in Stas and Jasper's game."

It was long. That's the part I understand. Well, no matter.
He doesn't have to discuss chess with me. Every city in Europe is full to bursting with people to help him analyze chess.

"I'm probably a better player than Jasper," he says.

This should all be good news, but Nikolai sounds miser-
able.

"As long as you don't tell him that," I say, "there's no
problem."

"He already knows," Nikolai says. "He has to. This is an

144

important tournament. No one would let someone with nothing to offer help them to prepare."

"So he knows," I say. "You've been able to help him. Why are you upset?"

"Because I didn't know," Nikolai says, standing up. "What else am I not seeing?"

"You're seeing it now," I say, feeling absurd. And a little bored. He's been graced. End of story. How much longer do we need to discuss this? I want to find Jasper and tell him I'm sorry he lost. I want to take my mother to San Trovaso. I want Italian lessons. I want to *eat* dessert.

"I have to see more than anybody else does," Nikolai says. "Before they do."

He's walking around in a tight little circle. I get up so I can follow him.

"It happens sometimes," I say.

"What does?" he asks.

"You mentally go past what you're ready for," I say, thinking of my last official meeting with André. "Then you catch up. And then you see. Like you are seeing now."

"It has to be better than that," he says.

"If it *has* to be, then it will," I tell him. "Just not yet."

"Salzburg is in less than a month," he says.

"Salzburg can't be what matters," I say. "All that can matter is how *you* are playing. It can't matter if someone is seeing more or playing better than you. It just can't."

He stops walking in his circle, so I stand still, watching him.

"No, you are right," he says. "It's just that I want to play my best. And if I can't see it until after the fact, then it is a disaster."

I take a breath. Notice that I am standing in fourth

position and move my feet. Right into first. How do normal people stand? I suppose I will know eventually. Back to the problem at hand. Another breath.

"Nikolai, you can't even care that you could be playing better," I say. "How you're playing is how you're playing. You will play really badly if you spend any time thinking about what you aren't doing."

I have no way of knowing if this is true for chess, but it is true in ballet. If you miss a turn or if your jump is not as high as you wanted, too bad for you. All there is is now. If your mind wanders either to the future or to the past, I am here to tell you that the dancing will suffer.

My thoughts have wandered. Nikolai's must not. I don't see how he would survive it.

"Of course," he says, sitting down. "I'm sorry. I never panic. Not in public."

"Don't be sorry," I say, my mind racing ahead to Salzburg. He has things to do. Suits to buy. Books to study. "Anyway, I'm not the public."

"No, of course," he says. "It's just I need to think of what to do now. How to proceed."

"You mean a plan," I say, knowing the only plan his big brain can hold is chess-related. This is what makes him incredibly interesting. And very limited. But still someone who matters to me.

"Yes," he says. "An entirely new one."

"Did he hit you?" It just slips out. But I have to know. I am more like Isabelle than I knew.

"Stas?"

"No, not Stas."

He is quiet for a while. And then for a long time.

"It's hard to explain," he says.

"Can you try?" I don't want to be mean or drain Nikolai's patience. Or his strength. But I need to know who his allies are. If his father can be reformed.

"He did, but only for five, six years. I'm taller than he is. I broke one of his ribs." Here Nikolai looks at me, shrugging and sounding puzzled. "It was an accident. A reflex. He actually laughed, although he must have been in considerable pain."

"It didn't upset you?" I ask. "Being treated like that?"

"He coached ice hockey," Nikolai says. "He grew champions. I knew what he wanted for me. I understood his methods were inadequate."

Huh. I will want to talk to Mama about this before deciding what I think. Or I may simply refrain from making a judgment until I understand what it is Nikolai thinks he understood.

"He hit my mother," Nikolai says. "That was much worse."

"Is that why she left?" I ask.

"Partly. Also, she thought chess would confine me," he says. "She was tired of fighting with him about it. She asked if I wanted to go with her, but I said no."

I don't have to ask why. His mother would not empower his game. His mother would free him to choose a life full of options. This is why we have mothers. To help us look at that choice. To force us to confront it.

"How old were you?" I ask.

"I hadn't won the under-eighteen championship yet," Nikolai says. "He hadn't even thought of leaving home yet. So when she left us, I must have been only ten or eleven."

"Do you miss him?" I know he misses her. I am sure he

147

wonders every day if he made the right decision. Only when he plays does he know he did.

"Yes," he says. "I do. But my chess is the better for his being gone."

That answers that. His chess will decide who his allies are. Father gone. Stas no longer necessary. There is only an onslaught of tournaments ahead. And the pressure.

"Isabelle and I weren't sure," I say, wanting him to know I had a good reason to bring the whole ugly topic up. "You know, if you did or—"

"Can you sit down?" he asks, interrupting me.

Sure. Yes. I can do this. I sit down.

"I have been better all summer," he says. "I have studied well and I have played beyond myself."

This is an improvement he will always have to report to those of us out here in life. How, otherwise, could we possibly tell?

"You have helped me," he says. "You have made things clear. Like glass."

I rather doubt this, as he has just complained bitterly that he is seeing things too late.

"What kind of things?" I ask. "What have I made clear?"

"Looking for Stas," he says. "Studying to play. Sharpness follows you."

Sharpness follows me. Here is a compliment I will take to the grave.

"Before she left, my mother gave me this," Nikolai says, his hands unclasping the thin chain he wears around his neck. "I want you to have it."

I let him put it on me. For the first time I think how *save and protect* could be a way to play chess. Not just a religious phrase.

"When you go, now part of me will always be with you," he says. "And in performance, you will be safe."

He doesn't know. I didn't take my farewell bow to him. Only to myself.

"I'm not going," I say. "Mama and Clarence have to work out the details, but I'm staying."

"But the Academy?"

"It's over," I say, peering closely, wondering if I can see the judgment I believe he will have. But it's pleasure. Unmistakable. That serene concentration he has when he studies settles over us.

"So you could come to Salzburg," he says. "If you wanted to."

"Yes," I say. "I would want to. I will come."

I mean to do very well in school. Well enough so that rules regarding attendance will be bent just enough for a travel schedule related to tournaments. Well enough for me to learn when Russia became the Soviet Union. Well enough to judge my improvements in the way I used to let the mirror do.

"Thank you," Nikolai says. "That will be nice."

We sit on the bench in silence. I can tell he is reviewing Stas and Jasper's game. Move by move. All forty-three of them. Over and over, until he knows he understands it. I finger the pendant resting in the exaggerated hollow between my collarbones. He will want and need this back, but as I reach for it, his hand pulls lightly on my elbow.

"Please keep it," he says. "At some point, you will go."

Count on Nikolai, with his far-reaching vision, to arrive at this particular truth well before it is a fact. Part of me envies him. More of me is overjoyed that what we have in common is no longer two lives spent in pursuit of capturing the Brava.

acknowledgments

I am indebted to a variety of books on both chess and ballet. Some I owned for many years and some I sought out during the writing process. All were informative in different ways: *Winter Season: A Dancer's Journal* by Toni Bentley; *Writing in the Dark, Dancing in* The New Yorker by Arlene Croce; *Linares! A Journey into the Heart of Chess* by Dirk Jan ten Geuzendam; *I Remember Balanchine* by Francis Mason; *Prodigal Son* by Edward Villella; and *Searching for Bobby Fischer* and *Mortal Games: The Turbulent Genius of Garry Kasparov* by Fred Waitzkin.

I am grateful, as ever, to Aliyah Baruchin, Jeff Freymann-Weyr, and Margaret Raymo for their questions and comments.